# NOCTURNAL PURSUITS

## GLENN ROLFE

Encyclopocalypse Publications
www.encyclopocalypse.com

# Contents

# ORSON'S GAS N' GO

Staring through the dirt-covered, cracked window by the cash register, Orson Allister wished he could give the flies buzzing around his head something sweet to feast on. It was hot as hell in the store, and sweat clung to him like a second skin. He was used to it, liked it even. His hand found the cold Budweiser he kept under the register. He found it helped him stay comfortable, maintain a good, solid buzz, and make the slow days, like today, tolerable.

Outside the blurry window, a Dodge Charger crawled from a plume of swirling dirt and dust and rolled up to the single gas pump out front. Orson licked his cracked lips and danced back and forth from one foot to the other. He closed his eyes and prayed out loud.

"Oh good God, please, God, let it be a nice little piece of ass. Big pretty eyes and big ol' titties. Please, please, please."

Giggling, he opened his eyes. They weren't teenage beauty queens, and they weren't yuppies. They were two rock n' roll rejects. Two guys—one in cutoff jean shorts and a plain white t-shirt, the other with long hair and a sleeveless jean jacket—stepped from the car. The long haired one by the pump threw his hands up and babbled at his companion. Orson couldn't hear them but understood the exasperated gesticulations. The tiny piece of plastic in Long Hair's hands told all. Fucking people these days with their Visa and American Express cards. Credit cards were all the rage, and he had to listen to every yuppie scum passing through whine and bitch.

He took another swig from the brown bottle before stuffing it back in place. The bells on the door jangled as the two men entered. He did his best to control himself. Being an eager beaver would lead to mistakes. "You have to take killing seriously," Daddy used to say. And he always had, just like dad. Kill 'em and grill 'em, or keep them someplace quiet where they could scream through the night and not bother a single nocturnal critter.

"Help you fellas with sumpin'?" he said.

"Yeah, update this shithole from nineteen-fucking-seventy, man," Long Hair laughed.

His cohort, Short-Shorts tried to hold back his own smirk, but Orson saw it clear as day.

Orson wiped his mouth with his sleeve and gave a small laugh. "Well, boys, I don't know 'bout all that. Make a livin' just fine as is. Ain't much, but she's all mine."

"Yeah, well you got a pump out there that needs an upgrade. It's 1987, man, people use plastic everywhere now. You're not gonna have this shitty business much longer if you don't heed that word of wisdom." Long Hair grabbed two six packs of Budweiser from the cooler and walked to the counter.

Short-Shorts meandered to the candy aisle. Little bastard pocketed two Snickers bars. Orson might be graying, might not be the smartest man that ever lived, but he had eyes like a hawk. He could spot a shoplifter in action every fucking time.

"Er, you boys headin' somewhere 'round this way," he said.

"You got a John?" Short-Shorts said.

Normally, he'd make 'em use the outhouse, but he had a plan for these two fuckers. "Sure do. It's back yonder, right of the last cooler."

"Thanks."

Orson glanced out the window.

Long Hair plopped the beer on the counter and slapped down a twenty-dollar bill.

Orson slipped one hand under the register and used the other to pat the money on the counter. "You see that there," he nodded at the big-breasted bikini model cut-out by the front door.

Long Hair craned his head toward the door. "Yeah, so?"

He turned back just in time for Orson to slam the claw end of the hammer into the top of his skull.

Orson let go of the handle and watched Long Hair stumble back. Blood poured down his forehead, splitting over his nose and trailing on either side of his lips. Orson slapped the counter and howled. He bit his hand to stifle his giddiness. Under the counter her snatched his hunting knife and scurried out around the counter, his slight limp providing the hitch in his step. Long Hair had fallen back on his ass and knocked over a display of Owl's Eye chips.

"Shhh, shhh, you just shut up. Just shut up," Orson whispered, his face inches from the dying man's. Long Hair stared into the void. He leaned back to see where the other man was.

"You just keep your mouth shut, yeah?" Grinning, Orson raised the knife above his head and stabbed it down into the dead man's chest. Half laughing, half growling as he drove the blade in over and over again, he only stopped when the toilet flushed.

Leaving the knife buried in Long Hair's chest, Orson crawled over to the edge of the front counter and reached around, fumbling through the box of goodies until his hand clenched around the handle of the hatchet.

"Hey, what the fuck, man. Sure looks like someone died in there. Now, it smells like it, too," Short-Shorts said.

A cooler door opened, beer bottles rattled.

"Hey, old dude, you still back there? If not, I'm just gonna take this shit."

Orson stood, the hatchet hidden at his side. Key in hand, he limped to the door and locked it.

"What the fuck?" Short-Shorts said, freezing in the candy aisle.

Orson turned, brow furrowed, his yellowed-chiclet teeth bared, and stalked the clueless asshole.

"Listen, man," Short-Shorts said, "you, ah, don't look so well. Just, ah, let me grab the beer and the gas and I'll get outta your hair."

Orson raised the hatchet.

"Hey, fuck, man."

Orson unleashed a growl and started for the candy aisle. His shoes slipped in Long Hair's blood, sending him into the shelves on the right.

Short-Shorts finally noticed the crimson pool spreading out before the register.

"Shit, fucking shit. Randy? You, you fucking…You killed…shit, man, just let me out. Please."

Orson steadied himself. He started grabbing bags of chips from the rack and throwing them at the man backing away from him. Short-Shorts ducked a few of the bags before reaching into the six-pack and chucking one of the brown bottles at Orson's head. It missed, smashing against the cooler behind him.

Orson wiped his mouth and said, "Now, don't you go doing that. You just calm down, hmmm? You just settle down."

"Fuck you, man. Get the fuck back."

Another bottle came hurling at Orson, bouncing off his shoulder and smashing on the floor.

"I told you to calm down, huh? You, you don't want to get yourself hurt now, right?" Before Orson could say another word, a third bottle smashed across his forehead, knocking him back into the chip rack

Short-Shorts raced for the door.

Orson felt blood spilling from the wound. It quickly obscured the vision from his right eye. Grabbing tight to the rack, he brought the hatchet up and sank it into Short-Shorts' shoulder. The man flung himself forward, toward the exit, taking the hatchet with him.

"Ahhh, Jesus," Short-Shorts cried from the floor. "You're fucking crazy."

"Now, you just watch what you say, huh? You ain't in no position to get sassy." Orson grabbed the knife handle, placed his foot on Long Hair's chest, and freed the blade.

Short-Shorts jumped to his feet. Back to the door, he reached up, pulled the axe from his shoulder, and threw it. Orson tried to sidestep the weapon, but it nicked him just above his already hindered eye. He flopped over onto the counter.

"Ow, ow, ow...you hit me. You hit me in the eye."

Short-Shorts turned and thrashed the door, kicking and screaming, throwing his good shoulder into it.

Orson dropped the knife, bent down, and snatched up the hatchet. The front door crashed open. Sunlight and hot, dust-filled wind swept in.

"No. No, you get back here." Orson chased him out into the light of day, nothing but murder on his mind.

Short-Shorts managed to get the Charger's driver's side door open as Orson came around the rear of the vehicle snarling. Orson swung the axe at the hand reaching over the lip of the open window to close the door. He hacked Short-Short's hand clean off at the wrist.

The man screamed as Orson wrenched the door open, reached inside, snagged him by the hair, and hauled him back out into the dirt lot.

"Please, please," Short-Shorts sputtered from the ground holding up his trembling good hand.

"I thought I told you to shut up," Orson said, casting his wiry shadow over the man's cowering form.

The *blat* of a big rig rumbling down the road stole Orson's attention.

Short-Shorts tried getting to his feet once more. He managed to stand just as Orson screeched and buried the hatchet into the back of his neck.

The sick thud-crunch spit blood, splattering it across the single, old-fashioned gas pump.

The big rig sailed by, shifting gears, groaning like a beast in the heat.

Orson had seen the eyes of the man at the wheel. He'd been seen. Rage swallowed him. Orson turned and began hacking away at Short-Shorts. Blood flung up at him, painting Orson's face, neck, shirt, and pants with each strike. After too many whacks at the hamburger mess he'd made of Short-Shorts' back, Orson kneeled next to the body and cast a glance at the brake lights of the tractor trailer sitting down the road.

A man in a cowboy hat stepped out.

Covered in blood, Orson waved.

The trucker climbed back into his rig. After a few seconds, the truck lurched forward, carrying on, away from the bloodied, grinning man.

***

Matt Farman grinded the trucks gears to shit. He'd been driving trucks for Ames department stores for two and half years and seen his share of fucked up and bizarre incidents, but the crazy, blood-covered asshole disappearing in his side mirror took the goddamn prize. Matt's hands were still shaking, his chapped lips trembling. He could feel the pulse in his throat throbbing like a parasite trying to beat its way through his flesh.

He'd stopped and gotten out, intending to help the man being attacking, but he couldn't force his feet to carry out the good deed. No way. The psychotic son of a bitch even waved. Nope, Matt wasn't that fucking stupid. You can't make sense out of the deranged. He'd jumped right back behind the wheel and Jesus H. Christ, he felt like the guy would rush upon him and appear at his window any moment.

He needed to get to the closest town and get the police. He cursed himself all the way into town for not getting his CB radio fixed. He vowed to rectify that as soon as heavenly possible.

The police station up on his left, Hargrove Ridge Police Department, looked like one of those trailers Matt had seen on construction sites, the ones the foreman hung out in. Two out-of-date, sky blue, Dodge Diplomats sat in the dirt parking area just outside the trailer's door. Matt pulled into the dirt and brown grass-covered field across from the station. Dust kicked up from his rig swirling around him as he opened the door and hopped down. The hair on the back of his neck stood rigid. The goose pimples marking his arms made his skin feel chilled despite the day's insane heat.

Becky's picture fell to the ground and flopped in the wind out into road.

"Shit."

He hurried after the picture and snatched it up before it had gotten too far.

Matt stared at the high school photo. They'd married right before he'd enrolled in truck driving school. She'd gotten pregnant but lost the baby a few weeks after he left. It was a loss they both pretended to be grateful for, while keeping down the hurt within.

Looking at her picture now, he wondered why he still cared. She'd cheated on him last year while he was away. Said she was lonely and how hard it was with him out on the road all the time.

He wiped the dirt from the photograph and stuck it back inside the cab.

She'd said she'd take him back. He knew he'd forgive her.

He closed the truck door and hurried across the deserted street. Passing the cruisers, he climbed the short set of stairs, reached for the station door, and nearly screamed as it burst outward.

"Holy shit," the mustache-wearing officer shouted. The man looked sturdy and mean as a rattlesnake. His two dark eyes squinted under a furious set of eyebrows. The name tag above his breast pocket read, Chief Gunter.

"Jesus Christ, man," the chief said. "Where in the hell did you come from?"

"I just saw a killing about five miles down the road, I think the place was called—"

"Orson's Gas N' Go," the chief said. "Lloyd," he shouted into the trailer. "C'mon, it looks like we finally got Allister. Let's go."

A smaller, older officer followed the chief as they ushered Matt over to the cruisers.

"Hop in," the chief said.

"What? I-I can't. I have to get to Denver by—"

"Sorry, buddy, not an option. You're my fucking witness, and if I have to bust you in the mouth and slap the cuffs on you, so be it. I ain't letting this motherfucker slip through my fingers again."

Matt was taken aback by the officer's threat. In a haze, he slipped into the cruiser's passenger seat as the chief shut the door after him. He didn't want to see the gas station, that psycho's face, or that messed-up scene ever again. And he sure as hell couldn't stick around in this desert shithole. Henry would rip him a new asshole if he didn't get his load to Denver on time. He'd already been delayed in New Orleans. For the moment, it didn't look like he had much of a choice.

The chief lit a cigarette, hit the gas, and hauled ass on the blacktop. No sirens, no further explanation, nothing but silence and secondhand smoke as the barren, Texas roadside flew by.

Sounded like this Chief Gunter had his suspicions about the loon at the gas station. Matt wondered how many times he'd done it before. How many folks had that psychopath murdered?

***

Orson knew Chief Gunter would be along any moment. Weren't the first time he'd been sloppy. Two years back, a couple claimed to have seen him dragging a body across the road. The old chief, Jed Williamson, showed up fifteen minutes later. He'd barely gotten away with that one. But that's why Orson kept the freezer stocked with fresh kills, mostly coyotes. He'd had just enough time to get one out there before Williamson showed up. Chief took one look at the coyote corpse and bought Orson's story that he'd shot the mangy animal and was just getting it off his property. Chief Williamson's young apprentice, Officer Gunter was a lot smarter than the old man. He hadn't stopped snooping around the gas station since.

Damn kid was like a bloodthirsty vampire waiting for night to fall. And sure enough, today's mistake might as well be Orson falling asleep in the yard with nasty gash on his neck. Yep, Gunter was starving and would no doubt be here any minute. Orson might have to produce a stake and put an end to that fucker.

Pulling at his hair, even ripping out a few patches, Orson peeked out the front door. He'd managed to cover up the blood with dirt from his basement, moved the Charger down yonder and slashed a back tire, but there was way too much blood at his little station.

"You really fucked this one up...mmm," he said, yanking out another chunk of hair, teetering back and forth, sweating like a whore riding a John into a soiled mattress.

The bodies of Long Hair and Short-Shorts were tucked away in the freezer. He'd have to get rid of them under the cover of night. Turning around, he grabbed the mop bucket and started on the store's floor.

"All I wanted was another pretty, big tittied lady, but no. Uh-uh, fuckers."

After a few minutes, satisfied that it didn't look like he'd slaughtered someone, he hurried down the aisle and into the bathroom, where he dumped the blood-drenched water. He removed the mop head and buried it in the cooler behind a stack of Busch beers.

Snatching up some rags and a bottle of bleach, he hurried out the door, squinting at the noon-high sun cooking the Texas dirt, and splashed a liberal amount of cleanser on the blood-spattered gas pump.

The glimmer down the road, kicking up dust as it raced in his direction, told him he'd better move quick.

***

Matt held onto the dash, unsure if he was more scared of the cop's high speed or returning to the murder scene. As the gas station came into sight, he knew without a doubt it was the latter.

"I'm not gonna have to get out, am I?' he said.

"You just sit tight, keep your panties on, and don't say shit unless I say."

*Prick.*

He kept the comment to himself. The anger fled as soon as they pulled off the road and into the gas station's dirt lot.

"Stay put," Chief Gunter said as he stepped out. He ducked his head back in. "And keep the door locked until I come back out."

The door slammed shut. Matt moved around the car, making sure the doors were locked.

Sitting back, sweating bullets as the sun cooked him through the windshield, he chewed his nails as he glanced around for signs of the lunatic.

The sports car and person he saw being attacked were also gone. He couldn't see through the dusty windows of the store. He imagined the whack job sitting in there, just waiting.

***

Orson flushed the bloody water down the toilet and returned the wash bucket to the space beneath the sink.

He stepped out just as Chief Gunter and his little buddy, Deputy Lloyd Gilbert, stepped inside. He looked back and saw a Phillips head screwdriver on the floor by the sink. He picked it up and tucked it in his back pocket.

"Orson, get your ass over here," Gunter said.

"Heh, heh, you boys caught me," he put his hands up. "Done near shit myself to death."

Neither officer laughed. He imagined driving his screwdriver through their eyes and smiled.

"Get your ass over here, Allister," Lloyd said.

"Oh, yes, I'm coming, I'm coming," he said, limping toward them.

"Got someone outside says they seen someone being attacked out front."

"Oh, is that...that so?" Orson said, he sidestepped the officers and headed for his counter.

"Hold it, right there." The chief pulled his gun from his hip and leveled it at Orson.

"Oh, hey, now...I ain't seen nothin', Chief. Don't you go pointing that at me, huh?"

"Shut it, and get over here, you sick fuck."

Orson fought the corners of his mouth, the anger boiling below the surface demanding release. His hand found the screwdriver in his back pocket.

"You got no reason for this, Chief. I ain't done nothing but sweat and shit here today."

"I said get over here." Gunter made a point to show Orson he'd switched the safety off his gun.

"Okay, okay, Chief. Don't shoot, huh?" Orson started toward them. His grip tightened on the screwdriver.

"Closer," Gunter said.

*Just what I was think—*

Gunter raised his gun and slammed it down into Orson's already wounded eye. Blackness swept across Orson's view. He hardly felt his body hit the floor before Gunter's boot kicked him in the jaw, rattling his brain.

"Jesus, Chief. What are you doin'?"

"Shut the fuck up, Lloyd. Go see what he was up to in that shitter back there."

"Chief?"

"Jesus, Lloyd, go, now!"

Orson moaned as Gunter dropped a knee onto his chest and grabbed his jaw. "I'm done fucking around. You're a goddamn killer, and I got me a witness out there who can testify. So, why don't you save me and Lloyd the trouble and tell me what you did with the fella you were bludgeoning out front half an hour ago."

"Puh-puh-please...I ain't—"

The butt of Gunter's gun slammed into Orson's cheekbone, his head slamming back against the floor. More stars came out to dance. Orson struggled to stay conscious.

"Nothing back here, Chief," Lloyd called out.

"Check the cooler, check the back. He's got something around there."

"Yes, sir."

"Don't fuck with me, Allister. It reeks of bleach in here, and I know you don't know shit about keeping a clean workspace. You're covered in your own piss and shit."

Orson heard the words, but they were muffled and far away. The weight lifted from his chest.

"Move and I'll blow your ignorant brains all over that floor." Gunter delivered a kick to his ribs, and then walked away.

"Nothing in the bathroom closet," Lloyd said, "but looky here. I moved this curtain and found a door with a padlock on it."

"Don't yammer on about it, get the fuck outta the way. Go check the cooler."

"Yes, sir."

Orson's thoughts floated back down from Mercury and Venus. He moved his hand beneath his leg and found the screwdriver again. He heard the beer cooler door open and close.

"You, fuckhead, you got the key for this?" Gunter shouted.

Orson didn't answer.

"Fuck it."

Orson heard two loud thumps, followed by the sound of the door to his cellar smacking the wall.

"I knew it," Gunter said. "Goddamn, I fuckin' knew it." Gunter stormed back over and lifted him from the floor. "Come on, you piece of shit. Let's go see what you got down in that basement of yours."

"Nothin' down there but extra storage and my bed."

"Shut up. Move it."

As they got to the edge of darkness, the wooden stairs disappearing into the black, Orson jerked back and grabbed the chief by his shirt, and then pulled him to the threshold.

"What the fuck do you think you're doing?" Gunter shouted.

Orson plunged the screwdriver between Gunter's ribs and heard the fight flee his breath in a gasp. "You-you go on and have a look, Chief."

Orson cackled as he shoved the chief forward and gave him a good, hard kick, grunting and laughing as he did so.

Orson ran his hands through his dirty hair as he listened to Chief Gunter's body thud and snap on its way down the steep set of stairs.

Hurrying back to the front register, Orson grabbed the baseball bat he kept behind the counter. Bending down, he grabbed another swig from the warm Budweiser sitting where he'd left it earlier. He wiped his mouth, ran his hand through his hair, and started for the cooler.

Rather than go in after Lloyd, he waited, bat clenched in his hands, giddy and trying not to get ahead of himself. There was still the witness. The truck driver was out in the car.

*After*, he told himself.

The cooler door opened.

"Nothing in here, Chief— Hey, what in the—" Lloyd reached for the gun at his hip but caught the fat end of the ash bat square in the middle of his forehead. He crumpled backwards into the cooler, the door closing behind him.

Orson ripped the door open and, stepping over the smaller cop's body, swung the bat down and bashed his skull until there was nothing but mush from the man's nose up. He loved the wet smacks each blow produced.

Tired and lightheaded, the adrenaline fleeing as quick as it arrived, Orson slumped against the stack of twelve packs.

"Oh, you done messed it all up now." He tucked his greasy hair behind his ear and headed for the witness.

Orson grabbed a fresh can of beer on his way out the cooler. He popped the top, chugged it down, left the can on the front counter, and, bat in hand, exited the store.

***

"Oh, what the fuck?" Matt said, double checking the door locks as the psycho came toward the police car, holding a gore-covered baseball bat out before him like a samurai sword.

"You," the lunatic pointed and laughed. His cackle belonged in an insane asylum. It was a half-laugh, half-growl—full fucking crazy.

The madman rushed the car and began slamming the baseball bat against the hood, caving it in from the front.

"You shouldn't go talkin' about other people's business. You should learn about keeping your mouth shut."

The bat swung at the windshield and splintered the glass. Matt looked for car keys, a gun, pepper spray, anything he could use to fight his way out of this nightmare.

"I should have," he yelled back. "I should have minded my own business. I'm sorry," he cried out.

The lunatics face slammed up against the passenger window, his nose squished sideways, his mask of blood making him look more sinister. "I'm sorry, I'm sorry," he mocked. He backed up and kicked the door. "I'm sorry, I'm sorry," he chanted again and kicked.

Matt began to cry.

*I should have kept driving. Fucking cop asshole making me come back here.*

The passenger window smashed. Shards of glass exploded inward.

Matt climbed into the driver's seat and pulled his knees up below his chin as the psycho reached a trembling hand inside and unlocked the door.

The bastard giggled as he jabbed and prodded him with the baseball bat.

"No, no, please," Matt said.

"No, no, please, heh, heh. Mmm, you keep quiet now, huh?" The lunatic smiled. His voice suddenly gentle. "Now, come on out of there before someone sees us out here like this, huh?"

Matt spun, unlocked the driver's side door, and poured out into the lot.

***

Orson rushed around the back of the car. He needed to hurry up and get this one inside before the whole scene played out like the one with Short-Shorts. Last thing he needed was for a Texas State Trooper to happen by.

He rounded the car just in time to see the guy slip under the vehicle. Frustrated, he began swinging the bat and growling as he beat the hell out of every piece of the cruiser he could.

"Just let me go," the witness's voice cried out from under the vehicle. "I'll go back to town, and I'll get the fuck out of here. You'll never see me again. I swear to God."

"Oh, okay. Come on out and you can leave, okay?" Orson said.

He was really sweating now, and it was hard to see from his left eye. He wiped at the wound with his elbow. His head swooned. He was losing too much blood. If he didn't hurry this along, he might pass out.

Orson reached into the car and put it in neutral. It began to roll. Stepping back, he rested the bat on his shoulder.

"No, no..." the guy hiding beneath said.

The man was crawling, trying to keep pace with the car. Orson brought the bat down on his ankles. The man howled but kept moving. The car came to halt another foot or so, revealing the rest of the man's legs. Orson dropped the bat, grabbed the guy by the boots, and hauled him out into the sun.

A handful of dirt came at his face, a rock stinging his cheek. Orson unbuckled his belt, pulled it free of his pant loops, and began whipping the man trying to climb to his feet. The man cried out with each slap of the strap.

Orson laughed, grunted, and swung again.

He led the guy right to the front door of the store. When he got close enough, Orson kicked him into the door, while still raining down on him with the leather strap.

"Oh, be quiet now, huh? You don't want to cry. You don't want to do that," he said, striking him again.

He laughed and moaned, halting just long enough to open the door as the man sat up and tried to protect his face from any more abuse.

Orson came forward, knee-first, mashing the man's nose sideways and knocking him back, his head smacking down on the threshold.

Orson wasted no time. He slammed the door shut on the man's head. The thick crunch was followed by a wetter, squishier sound. Orson continued slamming the door against his skull until the body fell limp.

"There, there," he said, gasping for breath as he slumped down next to the body. "There, there. It's okay. We're gonna be all right now, you see?"

The sun was directly over them. The stretch of empty highway hazy in the heat.

He could taste his own blood. Licking his lips, he snorted an exhausted laugh.

This was the busiest his little store had been in ages.

# In the Basement of the Amazing Alex Cucumber

Growing up, you hear about the creeps and the perverts who kidnap women, or children, and imprison them in dark, dank basements. You hear about the jars of hands, fetuses, and brains. In Bentleyville, two towns over from Fort Wayne, we had Alex Cucumber. Strange last name, stranger family. Alex was the only child of parents who were themselves quite outrageously talented in many dark and enigmatic ways. Kids whispered about his mother being a vampire, though no evidence of the charge ever made its way public. His father was assumed to be her creator. They both disappeared in 1998, the summer before Alex's senior year at Bentleyville High School.

Alex, who bore a striking resemblance to the late Doors singer, Jim Morrison, wandered the streets of Bentleyville night after night. Though not even eighteen at the time, he was seen with one beautiful lady after another, going in and out of Danny's All-Night Diner, and the massive house he had to himself.

I was a senior myself three years later when I found an odd invitation—a black piece of construction paper with a red cut-out heart and glitter-written message inside—upon my windowsill. The message read:

*Nolan Lachance, your presence has been requested to join us at a party thrown by The Amazing Alex Cucumber. Come alone or bring a friend. See you this Saturday. 9 PM. Sharp!*

*— Bev*

I wasn't sure who Bev was, or when Alex Cucumber had established himself as "The Amazing," hell, I didn't think he was aware of my existence, but I couldn't deny that the situation had me intrigued. The Cucumber's house out on Haley Street sat behind a line of massive pines that held its secrets along with those of young Master Alex. Rumors at school spread throughout the years that he could levitate, that he could read or control minds, and that he got whatever he wanted. No one said no to Alex Cucumber. And now, what of this invitation? It was childish in its make-up, using construction paper and glitter? However odd, I could not resist the opportunity to be in the company of our town's strangest resident. I made up my mind the moment I finished reading its sparkled lettering that I was going, and my buddy, Devin, was going with me.

I called Dev the next morning, informing him of the party.

"What if I don't wanna go?" Dev said, his newborn baby sister crying in the background.

"What if the rumors are true and his place is filled to the brim with girls that look like Megan Fox?" I countered.

"What if the rumors are true and we end up strung up by our flesh and sacrificed to the Devil?" Dev had a little Floyd "Money" Mayweather in him, and he could counter anything.

"Listen, just go with me. If you get bad vibes, and you want to get the hell out of there, we'll leave."

"I don't know, Nolan. Why can't you just take Billy?"

Billy Katz was our third wheel. His parents had money and Billy had every game and console any teenager could ask for, but he was a nimrod, and pretty much useless in real world situations.

"Absolutely not," I said. "Billy would get me thrown out, or instantly cast as a lost cause the second I walked through the door with him."

"All right, I won't do that to you, but I want *total* stay-or-go power. If I get the creeps, we're out of there."

"Clash powers granted," I said, referencing Dev's favorite punk band. "We'll meet at seven at my house."

"Deal, but one other thing, why does it say *The Amazing* Alex Cucumber?" Dev asked.

I had wondered the same thing myself, but guessed it was a play on the rumors of his unique abilities. "Maybe he's putting on a magic show," I said.

***

Saturday seemed to take a month to arrive (even though it was only two days). I waited for Dev to show up as the night began to devour what remained of the day. Fall had come to northern Indiana all too soon. The damn cold coming off Lake Michigan, where rumor had it, Alex had washed his crimson hands after many nasty dates, wasn't doing us any favors. Leaves were changing colors, and the hard rains of the last week had forced them to the earth's floor. You would have thought it was Halloween already, not mid-September. Dev showed up on time, as always, dressed in a black Alkaline Trio hoodie and a pair of skinny jeans, or girl pants as I liked to refer to them.

"Got enough gel in your hair tonight?" I said, staring at the wet-looking spikes of black hair covering his head.

"Fuck you, Nolan. I agreed to go. I didn't agree to fancy myself up like that," he said, gesturing at my clothes.

I had on the pair of black slacks and the black button-up shirt my mom had bought me to attend my Grandpa Joe's funeral earlier this summer, and a fairly new pair of white Adidas. A white fedora Grandpa Joe had passed down to me finished off the "fancy" look, to which Dev was shaking his over-gelled head.

"I didn't say you had to, but I look like someone who wants to get laid, you look like a slacker-hipster going to a Fall Out Boy reunion gig."

"Double fuck you," he said, flipping me off with both hands.

"Okay, okay, I'm sorry. You don't have to do this—"

"You're damn right I don't," he said.

"But I appreciate you coming with me."

I watched him fend off a smile, and then saw his eyes dart off somewhere behind me.

"What?" I said, turning to the patch of trees and unruly bushes that served as the end of my property, and the beginning of old man Peterson's.

There was a brief rustling among a black pocket that looked as though it had been swallowed by the universe. I stood staring, my imagination attempting to get the best of me. *Alex, or one of his friends, is watching us to make sure we're on our way.* A few seconds later, Van Halen, my dad's fat gray cat, jumped from the black hole, and plopped down on his rump to lick his paws.

I turned back to Dev, smiling from relief as much as from excitement. "Let's get going."

***

There were no cars near the Cucumber residence, and Haley Street was devoid of any sense of life. It seemed even the crickets were holding their breath as we reached the driveway. I thought cars would be lined up down the road. Dev slowed down as we neared the line of pines that served as the home's fence.

"You sure you want to go in there?" he said.

I wasn't. "Yeah, of course."

I took the lead, taking us from the blacktop to the gravel driveway. The crunch beneath our feet gave way to the booming thump of music we should have been able to hear from a mile away. There had been nothing until we crossed onto the Cucumber property and found ourselves standing before the impressive estate. I'd seen the home in the light of day (Gina Colby had dared me to go up to the porch earlier this summer. I did and was rewarded with a make-out session and handjob later that night). Standing before it under a pitch-black sky, the clouds casting out the moon as if it were uninvited by the amazing one himself, I got goose bumps, like the zits that greeted me on my fourteenth birthday, upon the canvas of my flesh. I passed off the fluttering in my guts as positive anxiousness.

"I'm following you, man. You ready?" Dev said.

I looked at my watch—it was not yet nine—and then around once more, searching the scene for signs of *anybody* else: cars, voices, *lights*. Despite the music, the sprawling three-story house was in complete darkness. "Let's hang back a minute. We're a little early."

"And what, stare at the grass, or the tree-fence? Fuck it, dude, let's go," he said, blowing past me and heading straight for the porch. "Whoa," Devin said, and stopped in his tracks. There was a shadowy figure standing on the steps. "Tell me you see that," Dev whispered from the side of his mouth.

I did but couldn't make out whether it was a man or a woman.

"What should we do," Dev whispered again.

*Run, run while we can. Get the hell away from this godforsaken place before we end up in the headlines as two missing teenagers.*

Instead, I stepped forward. "Hello, we're here to see Alex—I mean, The Amazing Alex Cucumber."

"Invitation," the voice behind us said.

I nearly catapulted out of my skin, and noticed Dev do the same as I spun around. A tall woman, clothed in a long, black dress that hugged every one of her curves, stood with her hands behind her back.

I hadn't brought the invitation with me and said so. "I didn't bring it. It didn't say to."

She took a minute to look us over, first Dev, and then me; her face was expressionless. Despite her awe-inspiring beauty, with high cheek bones, full lips, and her dark, come-hither eyes, I found myself repulsed by her. The urge to flee swam over me again.

She gazed past us, and then back to me. "Come, The Amazing Alex Cucumber welcomes you." She moved between us and led us to the porch. I searched for the shadowy figure but found the dark space empty.

The large, wraparound porch was shadowy and vacant. No chairs, no knickknacks, no welcome mat. The lady in black pushed the door open. The foyer within, bathed in dim-red light, was also empty of any possession. The walls were bare, or so I thought. A few steps in, a portrait hung near the bottom of the staircase across the room. As we got closer, I saw it was a family portrait. Alex sat between his mother and father. His mom on his left was smiling with her mouth closed; his father, on his right, was wearing a thin moustache on a stoic face with handsome features.

"This way," the lady in black said.

The staircase, from what I could make out in the red light, looked like it was carpeted in dark velvet—either blue or red— and rose to a second floor that seemed impossibly far away. The house looked humungous from the outside but seemed oddly larger on the inside. *It's probably the lack of furnishings; Mom says that really opens the space.*

Dev trailed behind, and he seemed much more comfortable than me. He kept poking me and grinning at the lady in black's ass. Of course, I noticed, but I was also aware of the heavy silence pressing down upon us when we should have been assailed with thumping music that had been audible from the driveway.

We reached the top of the stairs, where our hostess led us through a large, white door. Once open, the music with the pounding bass blared out. Mixed in were moans, whether of pleasure, pain, or both, I could not discern. Another red light was the only source of luminance in this room, as well. There were bodies moving everywhere. Men and women were swaying and grinding all around us as we followed the tall woman in the curvy dress through the center of the room. I glanced back at Devin—his eyes looked black in the red light—and saw him grinning. He was under the spell; I felt sick.

We exited the red-light dance floor and followed our mysterious hostess to a hallway lit by candlelight. The walls were bare here, too. The wooden floor squeaked at every step. I wondered if it would hold our combined weight.

"Where are we going?" I said.

She did not answer.

The hallway ended at an elevator. Strange, but true.

*Bing.*

She stepped aside and motioned for us to enter. The voice in my head warned me not to go in.

"Aren't you coming?" Devin said, once we were both inside. Our hostess, standing in the hall of candles, smiled, but offered no verbal response. Her creep factor was at about a nine. The door closed, and the elevator began its descent.

"Why the hell did we go upstairs to get into an elevator to go back down?" I said.

"Beats me, but did you see the friggin' shit going on in that dance room?" Dev bit his knuckle. "Holy shit, if that's what's happening up here, I wonder what we're heading into."

I wished he hadn't asked.

"Hey man, are you all right? You asked me to come, and now you look like you wanna go home and suck your mother's tit. What's up?"

I didn't feel right. *This* didn't feel right. "I-I don't think we—"

*Bing.*

The door slid open. On the other side was a wooden door.

"Now what the fuck is this?" Dev said.

I didn't want to find out. I'd had enough. I no longer felt the spine-tingling sense of mystery and wonder the invite had given me. I looked for the elevator buttons, wanting to go back the way we came, and found none.

Dev stepped out into the small, torch-lit foyer. I followed, chewing at my thumbnail the way I always did when we were at Dev's house watching Halloween or Friday the 13th. I wished this was a movie. The door looked like something that belonged on a dungeon in some medieval black and white film. It looked older than the rest of the house. The wood was worn, and also splintered in some places. It looked like there had been a slat to peep through at some point, but that had been covered and bolted with a rusted piece of metal. The door handle was a thick brass ring, which ran through the mouth of a freaky-looking demon gargoyle. I was certain that if we passed through that door, we were either going to enter a wormhole or head straight into Hades.

"Are we supposed to knock?" Dev said.

"Uh, I don't know. They must be expecting us, right? Your girlfriend wouldn't have sent us down here otherwise."

"I wish that was my girlfriend," he said. "I'm gonna knock."

He stepped up and wrapped his knuckles against the wooden door three times. The sound died on impact. The smells of the room began to present themselves—mildew, rot, and something that reminded me of *raw hamburger.* Combined with our elongated shadows cast beside the demon doorknob from the dancing flames behind us, the atmosphere was seeping into my blood stream like a narcotic. My affected brain conjured up a parade of macabre images that would have fit in perfectly in the painting Mr. Adkins had shown us in art class. *The Garden of Earthly Delights*, I think. I can't remember the artist's name, but like it or not, my mind tunneled toward its darker corners

Dev moved forward, raising his hand to knock again.

I grabbed his wrist, no longer wishing to be acknowledged by whoever was down here, but the door opened. And I swear I shit my spine out right on the spot.

The room before us was lit by more candles and torches, and what their light cast upon was certainly more perverse than the sexually charged rave taking place above. There were people I didn't recognize, dressed in various leather-studded outfits, chewing on severed arms and hands, or devouring what looked like intestines or organs. Devin screamed, and so did I. Clutching one another, we stumbled away from the door back toward the elevator. Not one of the cannibalistic heathens looked our way, they just kept on *feeding*.

Two dark shadows flew at us. The next thing I knew, Devin and I were snatched up by the unseen hands of shadow people, pulled apart, and taken into the heart of the ghoulish scene. That's where were introduced to our host, The Amazing Alex Cucumber.

He was mesmerizing. Clad in leather pants, an open white shirt, and with his longish, brown curls, he looked like he could have stepped straight out of a Doors poster. Two devilish, nude girls writhed up and down his legs, groping at him, all while staring at me and Dev.

"Wine?" Alex said.

Two glasses, surrounded by black smoke, floated to our hands. I took mine, but held it, still trying to clear my head and figure out what the hell was going on. I glanced over and caught Devin sniffing the glass. He shrugged at me and threw the dark liquid down the hatch.

"It's okay, Nolan. Despite all that you have already seen, I assure you, it is only wine. Drink, please. Let the spirits unburden your mind."

He patted the girls on the head. The one on his right rose. He whispered in her ear. She stepped over to Devin, pressed her breasts to his chest, and kissed him. Taking him by the hand, the woman led him past Alex, and through a group of fornicating figures beyond. He never looked back. I held the wine glass, not yet convinced.

"Your friend will be fine. Come, Mr. Lachance, I wish to share something with you," Alex said, pulling up the other naked imp by her chin as she sucked on his thumb. I felt movement in the front of my pants. As if she noticed, the girl with the black lips smiled at me.

Alex led me past more sexual trysts; thankfully, there were no more cannibal sightings. I already doubted what I had seen, or what I *thought* I'd seen. Could it have been some sort of illusion by my host? I thought of the rumors at school, mind reading, levitating and in those few seconds, I worked hard to convince myself that's what it was—magic.

Ahead of me, Alex whispered to his mistress. She smiled back at me and wandered off to the right, vanishing into the shadows.

*A trick. Another trick. She couldn't have—*

"I suppose you're wondering why I invited you here tonight?" he said.

I continued following him, looking back to where the girl had disappeared. "Uh, yeah, I mean, I didn't know you—"

"Knew who you were?" he answered. "I know every beating heart that resides in Bentleyville." He stopped at a curtain. "Please, my friend, after you."

"I— Where's Devin?"

"Nolan, I hate to repeat myself," he said. I saw something that might be anger flare up in his twinkling eyes. "Your friend is fine." He placed a hand on my shoulder and nodded toward the black curtain.

A dreadful feeling crawled over my heart. I didn't believe him that Dev was all right, and I couldn't shake the darkness swallowing me as I was led onward, presumably, to my own private execution. As his hand gripped my shoulder, those thoughts became murky. I felt *off*, but better. His smile made me smile.

"Go on. This is where the real show is," he said.

I thought I'd sat down my glass of wine, but here it was. I brought it to my lips, downed its warm, bitter contents, and parted the curtains.

The basement stretched out on and on. The room Alex ushered me into was a village. There were youthful-looking men and women all sitting single file, ten rows wide, at least a dozen to a line. They were all directed toward the stage on the far side of the room. At the back of the stage, surrounded by red and black candles, were two thrones, and sitting in them, two skeletal forms.

*Mr. and Mrs. Cucumber.*

"Who are all of these people?" I said.

"They are the missing, the lost," he said, placing his hand upon my shoulder again, and looking me in the eyes. "The found."

I felt his power was intoxicating, seducing me.

"They were like you, Nolan. Now, they serve a much higher purpose. They are no longer chained to the world outside of these walls," he said, urging me forward. "Walk with me."

I had never felt so good in my life. My mind, my body, my blood tingled, and it was euphoric. And my host, Mr. Mojo Risin', The Amazing Alex Cucumber, continued his speech as he walked me to the stage. His voice spoke not of peace frogs or riders on a storm, but of belonging, and family.

"*They* offer money. They live by it, for it. They are only their possessions. Here...we have none. We reward your efforts with love, with companionship, with truth. What they have is fleeting. What they have are lies." Alex directed me up the steps. "Look," he continued once we stood before the congregation of youth. "Look at their faces. Do you see it?"

I did. Their eyes were upon me, each and every one, smiling. I couldn't recall what I was outside. I couldn't remember my family, my friends, my life. I searched the crowd of beautiful faces, and spotted someone familiar.

"Yes, you know that one," Alex said over my shoulder.

It was Gina. Gina Colby.

"She is one of many, much like you. She wandered through *their* regimented series of make-believe freedoms, thinking she was an individual. *We* open eyes here. *We* welcome those who have no idea they have been deceived by the world around them, pulled in by the technology, distracted from the real world...the old world. Here, our eyes are wide open,"

Alex turned me away from the crowd. I managed a smile at Gina before turning to something unexpected. Devin, being held under his arms by unseen hands, was naked and shivering. He looked at me, but he was no longer there. His lights were on, but someone had snuck him out the back door. I should have been scared, angry, sad...

"We ask only one thing of our new members," Alex said, handing me a knife. "A sacrifice."

I wanted to do it, but part of me resisted.

"Children see this world free of confinement. They haven't been told that ghosts are not real, so they see them. They are not yet confident that monsters cannot exist, so they fear them. They are handed lie upon lie by those they trust most. They are fed fantasies of a man who brings presents, a fairy who comes for lost teeth, and a bunny who carries eggs of candy. We only want to give back to you that which they have ripped away—your innocence, your truth."

There was a tin pail in front of Devin.

"One act of brutal truth and you can have it all back. Free yourself."

The knife was now in my right hand, the pail in my left. Neither had been there seconds before.

"Do it," Alex whispered in my ear.

I turned to ask him why Devin couldn't come, too, but Alex (or Jim as I saw him) was now standing at the edge of the stage with Gina Colby. His advice was repeated, chanted by the throng behind me.

*Do it, do it, do it...*

I tried to weigh my options, but my thoughts were drowned by the chanting voices.

*Do it, do it, do it...*

The next few seconds flashed past my eyes as if in a dream. I looked up at the godparents of this cellar dwelling movement; hollow sockets looked back, their skulls appearing to wear smiles, prodding me onward, and my hand with the blade out before me like that scene at the beginning of the first Halloween movie, then Devin's neck, spilling blood into the bucket.

My head spun like a top; my eyes fluttered as I fell into darkness.

***

I awoke to the sound of rain thrashing against my bedroom window, the same window where I had found the invitation from Bev, the lady in black. My head hammered away in unison with the wind whipping around in the gray world outside. I sat up, noticing the odd scent secreting from my slick, pale skin—mildew, like the cellar of The Amazing Alex Cucumber. A dream: it had to be a dream. Loud music burst to life from my right. Startled, I slammed my fist down on my alarm clock radio. I knew the song, as it was from one of my favorite movies: the one about lost boys that had nothing to do with Peter Pan. I noticed something on my wrist and followed its faint red trail down my forearm. It was blood, dried and staining my pale skin.

*Knock-knock-knock*

"Nolan, there's a girl here to see you," my mom's voice said from the other side of the door.

"Yeah, who is it?" I said, sounding like I'd downed a whiskey and broken glass concoction as I slipped out from beneath my covers, scratching at the red stain on my wrist.

"It's Gina. Gina Colby...from your school," my mom said. In my mind, I could see her holding the laundry basket with an ear cocked at my door. "She wanted me to let you know that *Beverly sent her*?"

I froze with my jeans halfway up my thighs, my mind flashing back to the events in the basement of The Amazing Alex Cucumber, to the words of the great one himself: *"We ask for one thing...a sacrifice."*

"Nolan?" my mother said. I watched the doorknob begin to turn.

Glancing down I saw the knife was once again in my hand.

"Nolan?" Gina's voice.

"Oh, hello dear. He should be right out," my mom said to her.

I knew what I had to do. Why Gina was here.

I pulled up my jeans and slid the knife behind my back.

"Mother, come in. I have something I want to show you."

***

My mother's blood was still warm, slicking my wrist and hand. Gina was wearing the same beautiful smile she had shared at Sunday school, all those years ago, when we were just victims of our parent's ignorance. She took my crimson hand in hers as we stepped over the bloody mess in my room and moved with swiftness and ease down the hall, and then out the door like a whisper on the wind. Unheard by most but cherished by the chosen. We were *his* chosen, The Amazing Alex Cucumber. Our liberation of a town undone by its own want for modern distractions had begun.

# THE DEAD BROTHER SITUATION

Brenda chased him to the door, the snow howling up a storm. He needed her to back the hell off. She didn't understand, he was doing this to keep them safe.

"Alan!" she shouted, though it was quickly muffled and snuffed to a whisper beneath the wind.

Ignoring her, he climbed behind the Suburban's wheel, put the truck into gear, and headed out of the driveway. He glimpsed her dropping to her knees in her housecoat.

She'd never understand.

She could never find out. It would ruin everything.

There was no Rick, no Carson, no Bryan. All his "friends" were bullshit. This was no weekend hunting trip, at least not the way she thought.

There would be plenty of tracking, plenty of blood, and if all went well, enough meat left over to feed them for the next couple of months. He'd been getting overzealous the last two outings and bringing home nothing but scraps. He told himself he was still in control. He was the beast, and the beast was him.

Alan. Shit, she didn't even know his real name. And the boy, well, the baby had something in his blood, something in the kid's DNA that she'd figure out sooner or later. The truth always reared its ugly head sooner or later, whether people wanted it to or not

He was very interested to see how that would all play out. Would the kid wolf out as a child? He sensed puberty would trigger it, but who the hell knew. Maybe it was like other traits and the damn mongrel in the boy would lie dormant until he had kids of his own.

Did he love them? It was a fair question. One he wasn't completely sure he could answer. He cared about them, but not above his own...issues. He'd always believed to love you must put those you care about above all else. So, in that scenario, no, he did not love them.

The Suburban plowed through the heavy snow pounding the little backwoods town roads. He never travelled in this kind of weather without his chains on. Brenda didn't realize he couldn't stay home, not without putting her or Nicholas's lives in danger.

He headed west.

These old roads were a disaster. Plows wouldn't make it out this way until morning at best. Still, he had no choice but to push on through. Two hours into the drive he found Canyonville Road and turned right. The cabin of one of his earliest victims was about a mile down the road, just off the lake. When he'd mutilated that man, Matthew Lacey, he'd worried someone would come looking. But he'd returned to the cabin numerous times over the past year and a half and no one had ever shown. The place remained untouched as far as he could tell. Lacey's stuff still filled the corners, but no one had come to claim it. He'd at least expected to find a bank notice about foreclosure, but it looked like Lacey must have owned the place outright.

When his headlights found the mailbox, he glanced up the drive to see if he could see any lights through the trees. He always did a drive by just in case. The snow looked to be about a foot high, but he was confident the truck would make it through, and per usual, the old home sat in perfect darkness.

Nick slowed the truck before pulling a U-turn and heading up the driveway. He only feared the vehicle wouldn't make it for a split second, but the chains caught and clawed their way to the foot of the stairs.

He'd left a good stack of wood inside last month and found it nice and dry against the far wall as he pushed through the door. He loaded the wood stove and got a good fire going. It was freezing, and he wouldn't be changing until sometime tomorrow. If he didn't heat this place up like Hades, he'd be dead by dawn.

Once the fire was stoked, he fetched his bags from the truck. He'd have to shovel the driveway, at least around his truck so he could swing it around and get back down to the road. But there was no sense taking on the arduous task now; the snow was supposed to fall until somewhere around four in the morning.

The hunger was with him. He'd packed four good-sized steaks and a pork loin that he'd found stuffed in the depths of their freezer.

He dug out the cooler of meats and pulled out two of the steaks. The scent of blood travelled up his nostrils and tickled something deep inside. Nick was salivating as he peeled back the cellophane, picked up the dripping hunk of meat, and bit into it.

He enjoyed every succulent piece, making a damn mess of his beard and his sweatshirt as he devoured the meal. Nick swallowed it down with four Budweisers. Filled and feeling the slightest touch of a buzz from the beers, he made sure to lock the door, tossed a few more logs in the fire, and laid down atop the sleeping bag he'd brought.

His dreams were filled of all the things he'd grown accustomed to on the nights before the change. Old haunts, old foes, old kills, but also the more jarring images of Brenda and Nicholas. He stirred in his sleep as the visions of their deaths at his hands served as reminders of why he left them every month.

When he awoke to the voice asking "Who the hell are you?" and having the business end of a rifle in his face, he tried his best to keep the smirk from his face.

"I asked you something, you son of a bitch," the man holding the gun said. "Who the hell are you, and what the fuck are you doing in my brother's cabin?"

Another man, about half a foot taller with a dirty looking peach-fuzz moustache chimed in, "The hell you smilin' about? Huh?"

"Shut up, Shea," the brother Lacey said. "I'll handle this."

Shea backed away with his hands up, and mumbled, "Sure, man, okay. Whatever."

Brother Lacey put a boot into Nick's ribs. "Get up," he ordered.

"Okay, fella. I'm getting up," Nick said.

"Do you know my brother?"

"And you are?" Nick asked, rising.

"Paul Lacey, but that don't fucking matter to your ass. Do you know my brother? Answer the damn question."

"You mind not aiming that thing at my face?" Nick said.

"You answer me, and I'll consider it."

"Fine, no. I don't know your brother."

"Then what the fuck are you doing in his house?"

"There hasn't been anyone here in months. I figured it would be cool if I just sort of camped out here while I was hunting."

"My brother's been missing going on two years. And by the looks of you, you've been here more than just last night. You know where my brother is?"

"I told you—"

"He heard what you fuckin' said, trespasser," Shea said.

Nick clenched his jaw and bit his tongue. This was all too good. He'd been wanting to unleash on some fucking assholes. Chasing down bear and moose and deer had its uses, but putting motherfuckers like this in their place, well, that fed a whole other beastly hunger.

"Matthew Lacey," Paul said, still aiming the rifle at his face. "This is his cabin. He came up here two winters back to do some huntin'.

Ain't been seen since. You know something, you better fucking spill it now or me and Shea here are gonna have to exercise some good ol' goddamn street justice."

"And why you got blood on your shirt?" Shea added.

Nick looked down at the stains on his gray sweatshirt. "Told you I was hunting. Had a little dinner last night. That okay with you?"

Shea stepped up to him and kneed him in the balls. Nick dropped to a knee and clenched his fists.

"Ah, ah," Paul said. "Don't even think about it."

Nick thought about it. He wished he could hulk out and bury his teeth into these fuckers. But the butt of the rifle smashed into his forehead and dropped him to his back. Before he could react, the butt came down hard again and caused the world to go black.

***

He awoke tied to the chair in the corner, stripped to his underwear. His head ached, but he knew it wouldn't be too long before these sons of bitches got what they had coming.

What did surprise him was that both Paul Lacey and his more than just friends buddy, Shea, were also stripping down.

"Hey, Paul," Shea said, "Looks like ol' bright eyes is coming to."

"Well, well, well," Paul said. "We were gonna wake you with a helluva surprise, but guess you get to see it coming."

The snickering both men let out sent a tendril of nausea into Nick's guts. No way. No fucking way was he winding up the fly in these Pulp Fiction wanna be motherfuckers' web. He knew he'd turn today, sooner than later he fucking hoped, but that slim chance of these assholes trying to fuck him before he could unleash upon them with great fury, well, it was slightly terrifying.

"You want a sneak peek?" Shea asked.

Nick tried to free his hands, but the ropes were too damn tight. He gritted his teeth and dropped his gaze to the floor as Shea pulled out his stiff cock and waved it back and forth.

"What's a matter, tough guy?" Paul asked. "You ain't afraid of a little dick are ya?"

"He looks hungry to me, Paul. What do you think, huh?" Shea said. "You want a last meal, trespasser?"

Paul charged across the room in his tightie whities and slapped Nick.

Nick tasted the blood from inside his cheek as Paul sunk his nails into his jawline and raised his chin.

"You got one last chance to tell me what happened to my brother," Paul said. "One. And if you keep this act up of "I just found this cabin," I'm gonna fuck the hell out of your ass until you're cryin' like a baby here on the floor. And then, after Shea has his way with you, and only then, will I put you out of your fucking misery and kill you dead."

"Where have you been?" Nick mumbled.

"What's that?" Pau said.

"Your brother's been dead almost two years now. How come you and your boyfriend are just showing up here now?"

"Motherfucker," Shea said stepping past Paul and hammering a right hook into Nick's face.

"Wait, wait!" Paul ordered. "Goddammit, Shea, fucking hold on."

Nick spat blood on the floor.

"You do know, don't you?" Paul said, his eyes wide, a flurry of rage flickering through them, like a wild fire coming to full blaze.

Nick nodded and smirked. "Yeah, I know what happened to him. I was there all right."

"Say it. Say it, you bastard," Paul said. His eyes were glistening.

Another shot from Shea mashed Nick's nose.

"Goddamn it, Shea," Paul said, shoving the asshole who still had his dick hanging out.

"What?" Shea said. "This asshole here just admitted to killing Matthew."

"I heard him, dickhead. Put your cock away."

Shea did as he was told. Nick thanked the Gods for small blessings. He was sick of looking at the loser's pecker.

"He said he was there," Paul said. "Ain't that right, bright eyes."

"Shit," Shea gasped. "He does have fucked up eyes. What's up with that? They didn't look like that a minute ago."

Nick knew what Shea was talking about. He could feel the first hints of his other side. The way his blood surged to his muscles. He smelled intimate things he didn't care for coming off these two hillbilly perverts. He heard their quickened heartbeats, sensed leeriness. They noticed the changing tides.

"Fuck," Paul said, "who gives a shit about his eyes." He stepped to Nick, pulled his head back with a handful of his hair and said, "Now, I wanna here it outta your grinning mouth. Say it."

Nick nodded again. "Yeah, I was there."

"And?" Paul asked.

Nick stared Paul in the eyes. "And I ripped his fucking throat out and ate what was left."

The rage faltered in Paul's gaze. His eyes widened; awareness on some deeper level clicked into place.

Shea looked from Paul to Nick and back to Paul again, like a child who wasn't sure how to react or what to do in a suddenly dangerous situation.

And this situation certainly was fucked.

"Shea," Paul said, letting go of Nick's head, and beginning to ease away. "Get my rifle."

Nick inhaled deeply through his nose. As he did, his muscles rippled beneath the flesh. His shoulders gave an audible crack, like a fresh branch being stepped on, followed by something that sounded like grinding teeth.

"Hey, shit," Shea muttered.

His breathing became heavy, grunts accompanied his hollow laughter.

"G-g-get my g-gun," Paul said, his voice barely above a whisper, but Nick heard it loud and clear. Fear. These pussies were about sixty seconds from pissing their stained undies.

Nick's jaw snapped as he began jerking his head from side to side. His gums ached as the teeth dropped to the hardwood floor in a rain of enamel and blood.

"Jesus fuck!" Shea said. He'd yet to make a move for Paul's weapon.

Nick's body tensed and grew, popping, snapping, grinding into his werewolf form. His face went tight. His snout pushed forth from his nasal cavity. Black hairs slid from their dormant home below his skin. His clawed hands snapped free of his bindings.

The two men trembled before him. Shea yellowed his undies, his piss flowing to the floor. Paul cried out a high whine before turning for his gun.

Fully transformed, Nick kicked the chair free from his feet and launched at Shea, swiping upward and eviscerating the weasel from navel to chin. Shea's body flew across the room, slamming against the wall where he collapsed dead to the floor, his innards spilling out in a pool of crimson. His hands twitched as his pathetic mind was cast into the great beyond.

"You're a-ah-ah-you-you're a wer..." Paul sputtered. The gun, forgotten in his arms, may as well have been a stuffy from his childhood. He dropped it to the floor with a thud that was swallowed by the guttural sound emanating from the creature that stood before him.

"Puh, puh, please... I don't want to d-d-die," he whined.

Nick reveled in the beast's power. Felt it vibrating through his body, his muscles, his veins. He'd never driven a classic sports car, but he imagined the thrill coursing beneath the black fur was something akin to sitting behind the wheel of a souped-up Charger or Mustang. It was intoxicating. He revved his engines, his growl growing in volume, his hulking body flexing before the coward piece of shit dissolving before him.

Paul's wide eyes slimmed.

Nick welcomed the asshole's momentary bravery with a garish smirk, being sure to show the man his set of flesh-rending teeth.

Paul dropped to his knees and snatched up the rifle. He had it up and aimed directly at Nick's chest as the beast sidestepped the well-placed trajectory. One swing of his claws severed the arm holding the weapon and sent it to the floor. The weapon discharged as it hit the ground. Nick grabbed Paul by the throat and lifted him so that they were eye to eye. He could see the beast's yellow orbs reflecting in this poor fuck's watery eyes.

Nick sunk his claws into the man's flesh until the blood began to overflow from the wound and dripped from his fur to the hardwood floor in a crimson dribble.

Paul's eyes gave into the inevitable. His feet twitched then stopped. Satisfied, Nick slammed the dead man down and sunk his mouth into his chest.

He'd devoured much of the two weaselly men before bursting out into the dying light of the day and chasing down any other unfortunate creatures in the vicinity.

The two men were enough, but when you only got out once a month, gorging yourself on fresh meat was essential.

***

The next morning, Nick awoke inside the cabin. Naked and freezing, covered in the crimson delights of his latest hunt, he climbed to his feet and shivered. Gazing around the weekend home that had served him well, sheltering him and giving him a camp for his beastly adventures, he knew it was time to turn the page. The remains around him were more work than he felt like dealing with this morning. He would burn the place to the ground.

Forty minutes later, dressed and standing at the tail of his Suburban, he smiled as he warmed himself before the conflagration rising high in the sky, dancing with black smoke. It had been more than a year since he'd killed a man. The ecstasy it produced was incomparable. And if he was going to return his sights to the most dangerous game, there was one place he had to go, and one man he had to pay a visit to, for old time's sake

He walked around the truck and climbed in behind the wheel.

Driving away, the raging fire in his rearview mirror, Nick knew where he was going on his next hunt.

There was unfinished business in a little town called Gilson Creek.

He'd figure out what to tell Brenda, if he told her anything at all. There was such a thing as fate. Nick believed in it full heartedly. And his fate was waiting for him farther south in a place that he'd last seen slicked in blood and rain.

# Gone Away

Parting this way is not sweet sorrow. It's not sweet anything. Not even close. What it is is a thick needle through the glistening eyeball of your heart. Watching a child once so full of life and joy and the purest happiness this shitty universe has to offer be stricken with something so ugly, it is the epitome of devastation.

He wasn't even old enough to tell us what he wanted to be when he grew up. He was Marshall the firefighting dog from Paw Patrol one minute and Leonardo from Teenage Mutant Ninja Turtles the next, his just blossoming vocabulary suddenly stunted. *Mama, Dadda, Mimi, juice, candy, nuggies* remained even as the rest slipped away. Walking turned back to stumbling to crawling and now rests at attempts at rolling from side to side.

I watch my wife weep into her pillow. I see Mimi, my wife's mom, her eyes constantly gleaming, a hand permanently at lips that tremble when she thinks neither my wife nor I are looking. And even though a part of my mind, a slice of my heart wants to comfort them and be the ground to catch their fall, I can't. I just fucking can't. Call it selfish, but I can't get past my own hurt inevitably gearing up, building like the threatening snowy cliffs above the Coquihalla Highway. There's an avalanche coming, and it will lay me to waste. With his dim light withering faster now, we are clinging for dear life. I don't think of anything but my boy and this impending doom. I know there's a world and a life beyond, but I can't take my eyes off of his. And I can't contemplate time and space on this plane after it all comes down.

***

I woke up, like every morning before, not realizing I had allowed myself to fall asleep, and found him wheezing. Somewhere beyond the barely dawn-lit room, the sun creeping across the floor with the promise of a day I'll never forget or move past, my wife and her mother are dreaming. A small voice urges me to go wake them before it's too late, but I can't. I won't leave his side.

"I'm right here," I say.

His eyes are open, but they are someplace else.

And I take his tiny hand in mine and hear the whitewash from above as it begins its monstrous collapse and heads for us at full speed. An unstoppable, unimaginable wall of pure cold death.

My tears are blurring my last visions of him, but I won't let go. I won't let go.

His breathing has ceased as my wife and her mother enter the room and burst.

My own cries come from the end of my soul and tear at my every fiber. I want so desperately to give in and let them swallow me. My wife or Mimi has taken him in their arms, away from me. My hand holds onto the ghost of his as I curl into a ball and weep.

It feels like eternity beneath the weight of the avalanche.

I hold him in my heart, what's left of it. Somehow, I'm still here.

# SOMETHING IN THE WATER

## 1

Cindy and Randy waded into the warm waters of Demora Lake.

"This is almost fucking paradise, babe," she said.

Randy held his balls as he waded in up to his waist. "Yeah, it's something all right. What the fuck is that smell?"

"Your dirty ass. How the fuck should I know?"

He hated it when she talked to him like that. Who the fuck did she think she was?

"Get in already," she said.

"I'm coming. Don't rush me."

"Don't let a little shrinkage slow you down." She made her way in deeper, turning to face him, reaching around her back and undoing her bikini top. She let the straps fall from her perfect pert breasts to the water.

Randy's smile spread for miles as he gained a case of sudden amnesia over the testicular challenge of the lake. "Oh, damn, Cindy."

She turned and dove into the lake before he could reach her.

Fog rolled off the water as he waited for her to surface. When she didn't come up, he tried to laugh off the unease creeping over him.

"Yeah, okay. Come on. This isn't funny."

He was about to go under to look for her when she exploded from the water behind him and wrapped her arms around his neck.

"Fuck!" he shouted, shoving her away.

"Oh, come on, Randy. Don't be such a fucking baby. I'm just messing with you.

"Don't call me a baby."

"Oh, sorry." She reached under the water and grabbed herself. "Don't be such a pussy."

She didn't have time to react as his fist flew to her nose and sent her backwards. She disappeared under the surface.

"Shit," Randy muttered. Now, she was gonna hate him. And God forbid if her father found out. The guy was a six-six mound of muscle and destruction waiting to happen, MMA vet and everything.

"Cindy?"

She was fucking with him again.

*Goddamn her.*

The thought occurred to him that he might have knocked her unconscious and she might be drowning.

Randy hurried forward, reaching for her. His hands came up empty.

*Fuck!* If she was screwing around, he'd hit her again, her daddy be damned.

He went under the lake surface searching for her. She should have been right—

Something grazed his ribs. He screeched underwater and came up coughing out the water he'd swallowed.

"Randy," she said, startling him. She was bathed in the moonlight surrounded by the fog and the shadows. Something was wrong with her face. And it wasn't just the bloody nose he'd given her. The skin over her cheek...it was *bubbling*.

"Jesus, Cindy. What's wrong with your face?"

She touched the now oozing wounds with her fingertips. "What's wrong?" She pulled her hand away, a web of something mucus-like trailing from her fingers.

"Oh fuck." Backing away, Randy noticed the bubbly oozing shit was moving, inching its way across the bridge of her nose. He watched as Cindy raised her hand and stared at the viscous sludge slowly dripping from her fingers to the water.

"What is it, Randy? What the hell is it?"

"Get back," he shouted.

"Randy?"

"I mean it, Cindy. Don't fucking touch me."

"Randy?" She suddenly doubled over, covering her eyes with her arm. Something moved across her face, crawling upward.

Her screams sparked him into a full-on run. The water fought him. It was like he was moving in slow motion and he'd never get away. He glanced over his shoulder and instantly wished he hadn't.

In the moonlight shining down upon her as if it were a spotlight, her arms reached to the heavens along with her cries for help. He saw tiny things writhing from the wounds on her eyes, nose, and cheeks.

*Fucking gross.*

She dropped beneath the surface and out of sight.

"Shit. Fucking hell." Randy hurried toward the shore. He hit the rocky sand and kept on trucking until he felt them. He was nearly to his Plymouth when he dared a glance at his legs.

His scrawny pasty-white chicken legs were writhing with the fungal horrors from the lake.

He didn't dare touch the disgusting splotches with his hands. He'd seen them spread on Cindy. Looking to his car, he got a bad idea. He hurried to his door, reached though the open window, and tugged the trunk latch. Moving around to the back of the vehicle walking stiffly like his legs were wooden stilts, he reached for the red gas can. He didn't know if it would have any effect on the things crawling over his flesh, but it was his only option.

Randy uncapped the can and began to douse his thighs, knees, calves, and feet with gasoline. The burn was instant. He gritted his teeth and finished emptying the fuel before tossing the can to the ground and falling against the back of his car.

Clenching his eyes shut against the pain, praying the skin on his legs wasn't being eaten away, he stood his ground as long as he could. He felt dizzy and clammy, but he held on, waiting for the gas to hopefully work its magic. When he finally dared a look, he smiled, despite the awful burning over his legs.

At his feet, several puddles of whatever had attached to him from the lake, lie dormant.

He didn't scream until he saw the patches of missing skin. Where the writhing masses had appeared on his legs were weeping blotches of raw muscle and tissue, the flesh completely gone.

He was starting for his driver's side door when he saw the thing stepping from the water.

"Cindy?" he said, weakly.

The shape was hers, but something was horribly wrong.

"Oh, fuck this." He climbed in behind the wheel, stabbing the keys into the ignition. The Plymouth roared to life just as the shape reached his window.

"Jesus!" he cried.

An appendage that was nothing more than a mass of the bubbling, writhing fungus reached in and slithered its way down Randy's screaming throat.

Gagging and hysterical, Randy stamped the gas pedal as his flailing right arm pulled the lever that put the car in DRIVE.

The Plymouth shot forward. He could still feel the things moving in his mouth across his tongue and moving down his throat as the car crashed through thickets smacked off a few smaller saplings and dropped down over the embankment and into the lake.

Randy Plourde was dead within minutes, his car half in and half out of the lake.

The thing that had been Cindy Thomas crumbled into various piles of the fungus that had devoured her tissue and muscle. The fungus finished what gristle and organs remained from the girl before receding back into the warm waters.


# 2


Christopher Lothridge and his best friend, Steve Sholz, headed out beneath the starry night sky into the peaceful waters of the lake Steve had been raving about over the last five years. Steve was in his mid-sixties. Chris turned thirty last October. Despite the age difference, the two got along like peas in a pod, and there was a slight father-son dynamic. Chris had never known his dad—the old man left home before Chris had gotten out of diapers. Chris had worked alongside Steve for half a decade now at a hotel in Augusta. Over the years, he'd leaned on the man for support and advice on everything from girls to plumbing, and even how to propose to his fiancée... Well, ex- fiancée now, but the old man's wisdom and friendship was Chris's most valued commodity next to his mother.

"You sure there's fish here?" Chris said as he paddled the oar through the water. "It fucking stinks."

"That's just your ass. Of course there's fish, probably bigger than anything you ever dreamed about catching." Steve opened the cooler and grabbed two Budweisers. He uncapped the bottles and set one into one of the little cupholders he'd installed himself next to Chris's lap. After a good guzzle, he gave an emphatic "ah" and wiped his mouth with the back of his meaty forearm.

"I'm serious," Chris said. "It smells awful. You sure this isn't where the city ditches their waste?"

Steve leaned toward the surface of the lake and gave it a couple big whiffs. "Well, it ain't your wife's coochie, but it does have a bit of a punch to it, huh?"

"Yeah, yeah, yeah," Chris said, taking a break from paddling and snatching up his ice-cold beer. "I don't know if I wanna eat anything we catch out of here."

"I don't remember it smelling like this," Steve said. "Maybe they did start putting shit into it."

Steve straightened and lifted his ballcap. The moonlight shined off his bald head.

"What do you wanna do?" Chris asked.

"Well, we're all the way out here, ain't we? Might as well do some fishing. We can just do some catch and release, I guess."

"Better than nothing, I suppose."

Steve grabbed an oar and began paddling them farther out.

Chris looked around. It was beautiful out here. A clear night sky twinkling with stars and the air was a comfortable sixty-eight degrees. It had been in the upper seventies for the last couple of days, and the lakes should all be nearing perfect swimming temperatures soon. It was early June still, but a warm Maine spring should have ponds and lakes such as this filled to the brim with beachgoers by next weekend. Maybe not this body of water—hell, it did smell something wicked. Could it be the warm spring? Maybe the algae were worse than normal? Could algae smell so rank?

"Here's good." Steve placed the oar back into the boat and reached for his fishing rod. "Make yourself useful and hand me my tacklebox."

"What are you using, old man?"

Steve took the box, set it down, opened it up, and picked up a dangly lure.

"A jig?" Chris said. "You gotta be kidding me. Come on."

He laughed as he watched Steve attach his lure. He watched the man's shaky hands work twice as hard to get it set. When he finished, he looked at Chris. "Boy, you gonna just sit there and watch me all night? You ain'y getting' weird on me, are ya?"

After a second, Chris grabbed the plastic container. He popped the top and pulled out a nightcrawler.

"Oh, jeesh," Steve said. "Worms?"

"Hey, let's just see who gets the first bite."

They each faced in opposite directions, casting out into the calm, stinky water.

Chris wondered if they'd catch a fish with three eyes or hook the creature from the Black Lagoon.

Silence fell over the night like a shadow in the dark, subtle and full. Chris tugged his line, let it rest, and tugged again. He was thinking about Steve's shaky hands and wondering if he should say something, ask if it was something serious when he felt the jerk from the water.

"Hey, hey," he said. "Beat ya, old man."

"Not so fast, boy," Steve replied. "I got a friggin' whopper over here."

*Oh, no you don't, old man,* Chris thought. No way was he losing this one.

"Ha! Holy hell," Steve shouted.

"What? You too weak and feeble to haul that big boy in?" Chris asked.

"Uh," Steve moaned.

"Steve?"

Chris looked over his shoulder to check on him when he felt the small boat sway and heard the splash as Steve went into the water. Chris lost his balance, tried to catch himself at the little boat's edge, and caused the damn thing to capsize as he fell and lost his rod. He was splashing in the lake before he knew what the hell had happened.

He had something in his eyes as he came up for air. "Steve! Steve!"

The old man cried out once and fell silent.

"Steve!"

Chris wiped at his eyes, trying to clear them so he could find his friend.

*Jesus, what if he's had a heart attack.*

He'd managed to clear away whatever was clinging to his eyelashes. The shit felt like the gunk that came with a bad case of pink eye. Looking around, the fog coming off the water, the stench clinging to everything including the air, he made out the upturned boat, but no Steve.

He dove under, unable to make out a damn thing below the surface. After coming up for air and another check for his friend, he dove back in going beneath the boat and grabbed hold. He managed to get one side out of the water and kicked like crazy as it moved farther into the air.

"Come on," he shouted.

As the boat flopped down the other way, splashing into the water, he scrambled up over the side and crashed to the floor. He hurried to his knees, glancing all around the boat, trying to ignore the burning in his eyes.

"Steve!"

The old man's orange life vest bobbed up to the surface.

He reached out over the edge, careful not to flip the boat again, and got hold of the life vest with the tips of his fingers. As he pulled it in, a hand shot up from the water and clasped around his wrist.

Instinct told him to pull Steve in, but when he noticed the pulsating flesh on the man's knuckles and the familiar face emerged, Chris screamed.

The moan his friend gave out in response was the worst sound he'd ever heard. Worse than the last gasp of breath his grandfather had taken in the sterile hospital room. Worse than the cry his best friend Rick Bonifant let out when he got his leg broken backwards at the

Cony High School State Championship game. The sound was filled with agony and helplessness. And Chris knew it was the essence of his friend, his mentor, the man who'd become his pseudo-dad crying out to the world one last time.

"Steve!" he called out again.

The half-face poking up from the lake was swallowed in wiggling bits of something that looked like mold on an old piece of bread. His one gray-blue eye disappeared under the migrating fungus. His moan choked off as lake water flooded his dissolving mouth.

Chris yanked his wrist free and fell back in the boat. He grabbed the oar and pulled it to his chest, clinging to it with everything he had left. Staring up at a perfect night sky filled with stars and promise, he wanted to be home. He wanted to be at Jonathan's bar having drinks with Steve, not cowering here on this fucking lake seeing the man's ruined face and those damn whatever they were crawling over him.

It was then he noticed the silence. Sitting up, he peered around the boat, searching for any signs of movement. Outside of a few bubbles and a couple of patches of foam on the lake's surface, all was still.

He straightened out in the boat, wiped the sweat and tears from his eyes, and gently placed the oar into the water. He waited to see if something would happen. When nothing did, he began to paddle his way back to shore.

His thoughts moved to Kim, Steve's wife of thirty-plus years. What the fuck was he supposed to tell her? How could he explain this? It was insane. Tears filled his eyes again blurring his sight. The spot where they'd set the boat in was just ahead.

He stopped paddling to clear his eyes as the boat continued to coast toward the bank. And it all hit him. Steve was gone. Taken into the lake by something he couldn't explain. The vision of his face— Chris set the oar down at his feet and sobbed in a way he hadn't since he was a child. His entire body hitched, wracked with soul crushing hurt. He buried his face in his hands and wept.

When his crying spell slowed, he reached down for the oar. He didn't notice the colorful fungi making their way to his hand. He was too lost in sorrow to feel their feather-light touch as they moved over his flesh.

The small boat made a thud as it hit the bank. It was nearly pitch black at this corner of the lake and the flashlights they'd brought with them were probably back there sinking below the surface. He tossed the oar ashore and latched his fingers into the grass, digging in to the dirt as best he could. He crawled out of the boat onto the grass and laid there for a second contemplating whether he should try and get the boat at least out of the water. He thought of Steve and decided against it. There was *nothing* worth braving the lake again.

On his feet, he reached into his pocket, grateful to find the keys to the truck still there. He hurried over to the vehicle and climbed behind the wheel. His clothes were wet, but he didn't give a shit. He was just happy to be getting away from here with his life.

The vehicle bumped and jostled its way over the dirt trail they'd driven in on. When he got to the blacktop of Old Belgrade Road, he put the pedal to the floor, letting the tires screech as he fishtailed it down the otherwise quiet back road. When the vehicle straightened, Chris began to laugh. It was an awful sound, the laughter of the mad, but he couldn't stop himself.

His vision grew blurry as he reached the junction to Route 3. He automatically wiped at his eyes. It wasn't until he felt something push its way under his eyelid that he began to panic. The sensation was what he imagined it might feel like to have someone force a wet Swedish Fish candy under there. His laughter turned to screams as he covered the eye and its wiggling invader with one hand and swerved back into his own lane.

There were more, many more of the lake fungus writhing on him now. He could feel them prickling his flesh on the backs of his hands and wrists. A tingling sensation made the right side of his face cold and numb. A sharp pain burst to life behind his infested eye.

Chris lurched forward in immense pain. He didn't see the bend in the road as the truck flew from the pavement and rumbled into the brush. He lifted his chin in time to see the front of his truck smash into the large tree.

His final thought: *Jesus fucking Christ, please take me now!*

# 3

"Holy Fuck, Liza!" Grace couldn't believe they'd actually knocked someone out and put them in the trunk of her car.

"I'm driving," Liza said. "You cool with that?"

"Yeah, fuck yeah," she said.

Grace stared in awe at her best friend as she put the Volkswagen in gear, squawking the tires down the street away from Granite Hill Fitness Center.

"Aroooo," Grace howled out the open passenger side window. She never believed in the push and pull of lunar cycles, but the full moon in the otherwise pitch-black night called to her.

"Don't you just feel so fucking alive?" Liza said as she shifted gears and stamped the pedal to the floor.

The girls went screaming down the backroad heading toward their destination.

"So, do you, like, have some crazy plans for him?" Grace asked.

Liza drove the car down a dirt road.

"Oh, hell yeah. He's going to wish he'd never fucked with this bitch."

Grace had warned Liza about Trevor. A rich, pretty boy gym rat who cared more about his abs and his hair than any relationship. Liza thought she had him under her spell, but Grace knew better. Mr.

Hotness had given her a case of herpes and ditched her ass cold two days ago.

The car came to a stop. Liza rushed out without a word. They were surrounded by hemlocks rising up into the night like the arms of burnt and scarred ancient gods. Grace stepped from the car and joined Liza at the trunk.

"Hold this," Liza said, handing her a pistol.

It was heavy, real. It felt...good. Grace took three steps back and aimed the barrel at the trunk.

Liza opened it.

Trevor struggled against the zip ties Liza had strapped him with. She reached in and pulled the duct tape from his mouth.

"You fucking bitch," he said. "What the fuck do you think you're doing? Huh?"

"You gave me something nice to remember you by and I just wanted to return the favor."

She reached in for him as he tucked his knees to his chest and kicked her in the face. Liza flopped over backwards, blood running from her nose like a river down her mouth and chin. She wiped the blood away with the bottom of her shirt.

"Come on, bitch. Come get some more."

"Shoot him," Liza said.

"Wait, what?" Trevor asked.

Grace looked to Liza.

"Aim for his legs."

"No, you wouldn't. Grace, no!"

Grace aimed left and fired. The report was deafening, but she felt a thrill surge though her as he screamed.

"You fucking shot me!"

Liza looked at the gun. "Stuff that in your jeans and help me get this piece of shit out."

Grace did as told.

Trevor squirmed but didn't fight them as they grabbed him under the arms and hauled him over the lip of the trunk. He hit the ground curling into a fetal position. "Please don't kill me. Please don't."

"Shut the fuck up," she said. "When I want you to beg, I'll fucking tell you." She turned to Grace. "There should be a nice spot in just a few hundred feet. Help me."

Grace hooked his other arm and they proceeded into the darkness. It was all totally beyond fucked up, but it was also empowering. They dragged Trevor whimpering and whining into the woods.

"Something stinks," Grace said.

"There's a lake out here," Liza said. The statement hung in the air.

"Whatever you're planning," Trevor said. "I'm fucking sorry, Liza. I'm so fucking sorry."

It was dark, but Grace heard the thud as Liza kicked Trevor in his wounded leg. His cry rang out through the quiet night.

"I told you to shut the fuck up," she said. "You deserve what you've got coming."

They stumbled, and fell, tumbling to the forest floor as the ground dropped down a good four feet.

"Jesus, Liza," Grace said. "What the hell was that?"

Up ahead, Grace saw the shape of a large rock standing alone in the clearing. Letting go of Trevor as he moaned on the ground, Grace pulled her cell phone from the pocket of her shorts and turned on her flashlight app.

Rising to her feet, she said, "What the fuck?"

Just ahead of them, it looked like a bulldozer had come through the middle of the woods and laid waste to every tree. The path started just behind them and was at least twenty feet wide. A large blackened thing sat up ahead where the path ended abruptly.

"What the fuck is that?" Liza asked.

"I don't know. You chose this spot. This wasn't here?"

"Na-ah," she said.

"Its...its...like, a meteor or something," Trevor whimpered from his spot on the ground.

Liza broke out of her trance to deliver another kick to his leg. "Fuck off."

Trevor moaned through gritted teeth.

"Maybe he's right," Grace said. She scanned their surroundings with the light. "Look at the trees near the path." Scorched leaves and branches lined each side of the track.

"What's over there?" Grace asked, shining the light off to the left.

"The lake," Liza said. Her nose was still bleeding.

"Well, it's either this thing up ahead that reeks or the lake," Grace said. "Maybe we should just take him somewhere else."

"Don't chicken out on me now," Liza said. "It stinks. So fucking what? We can do it right here."

"Yeah, okay, but maybe we do it a little quicker," she said.

"Hey," Trevor said. "What if I just keep my mouth shut and you guys just drop me off at the hospital? I don't wanna be out here with whatever that is." He nodded toward the meteor.

"You're more scared of *that*?" Liza pointed toward the large shape before kneeling next to him. "I'm the baddest bitch in these woods, mother fucker. *I'm* your goddamn nightmare. You hear me?" She pulled a large hunting knife from the sheath strapped to her lower leg and placed the edge of the blade to Trevor's cheek. "You always were so pretty."

"Liza, don't—" he started.

She pressed harder and then ripped the knife across his cheek from his temple to his jaw. He screamed as the blood began to flow.

She stood and watched. Grace spotlighted the event with her phone app.

"You're not going to screw over another girl for the rest of your pathetic life," Liza said, now stalking around him.

"My fucking face... Ahh!" he cried. "You...you..."

"Say it, mother fucker," she said. "Say it."

"BITCH!"

Liza lifted her leg and stomped his wounded leg.

"BITCH!"

"That's right," she said. "Say my fucking name."

This time, she stomped where she'd sliced his face. And she did it again and again.

She stepped away, hand clenching the knife, breathing heavy. The look in her eyes was one Grace had never seen in all their years together. It was a look she'd only witnessed in those nature shows about big cats about to strike their prey.

Trevor was blubbering as Liza grabbed the zip-tie around his ankles. "Come on," she said to Grace. "Put that thing away and help me."

Grace killed the app and slipped her phone into her back pocket. She joined Liza at his feet, grabbed hold, and helped haul him across the meteor ditch and toward the incline.

It took a little extra muscle, but together they managed to get him up and out of the path.

"Don't...don't..." he muttered.

Liza stayed silent.

As they got to the edge of the trees, the small beach and the lake came into view.

"We'll finish him out here," Liza said.

"*Finish* him?" Grace asked.

As they reached the rocky shore, Liza let go of his legs. "Yeah, don't tell me you think this piece of shit would actually keep his mouth shut."

"Well, I guess I didn't think about it, really."

"I will. I will, I swear it," he said.

This time it was Grace who kicked him.

Liza followed with another swift boot into the small of his back. "We let him go and this cheating, raping, disease sharing asshole will fly right to the police. And who are they gonna lock up? The rich ass white boy? Fuck no."

Grace knew she was right. It was in the news every other week, some white privilege shithead like Trevor got away with a slap on the fucking wrist while black kids were getting shot for wearing hoodies in the wrong neighborhoods. Getting threatened and accosted on their own property because they're the wrong fucking color.

"No, they're going to say I asked for this mother fucker's fucking herpes. That I revoked my right to say no when I smoked his goddamn weed. That I knew what I was getting into when I went to his house in the hills."

Grace had known about the STD, but she didn't know Trevor had raped her. She nodded. "Yeah, fuck this piece of shit." She pulled the handgun from her shorts. "Let me give him some more."

"NO!" he yelled.

"Go for it," Liza said.

Grace grabbed her phone with her other hand and handed it to Liza. The flashlight came to life. The blood from Trevor's face was all over his neck and chest.

"Fine, do it," he said through a mask of crimson. "You two little cunts are going to prison. They'll find out what you've done. You're too fucking stupid—"

BANG!

The bullet ripped through the right side of his chest just below his clavicle.

Trevor's wails ripped through the night.

Liza handed the phone to Grace and took her knife, jamming it into the hole Grace just made and twisting it in a circular motion like it was a spoon in a mixing bowl. "Scream, mother fucker. There's no one to hear you."

Grace was about to take aim for another shot in his other leg when something wet and powerful clutched her forearm and yanked. The gun splashed in the water. A hellfire of pain flared in her shoulder as she spun with the flashlight to see what had happened.

Her arm was gone.

Grace shrieked.

The massive shape beside Grace smelled like a rotten bag of potatoes. It stood nearly seven feet tall and wore a mask of some sort. It was also wearing a dark metal chest protector. Without thinking about it, Grace tried to pull the trigger of the gun she no longer held with the arm that was no longer there.

The thing lashed out and backhanded her. Everything went black.

***

Liza heard Trevor screaming as she backed away. This fucking space monster had just ripped her best friend's arm off. She watched in shock as it bent down and picked Trevor up as if he were a toddler. Trevor's cries echoed over the lake. The space creature matched Trevor's wail with a roar of its own.

It spun around and threw Trevor through the air and into the lake along with Grace's arm before turning its full attention to Liza.

Trevor rose from the lake, the water line coming up under his chest. His cries were filled with horror, the sounds of someone being murdered. Although she'd come here with murder on her mind, his screams scared her to her core.

There were no words in the garbled cries coming from him as he fell face first into the waters. This time, he stayed below.

Liza turned to run, but the monster snatched her hair and pulled her into its clutches. She couldn't make out many details in the moonlight, but as it wrapped its slimy hands around her arms, she noticed a chunk of its upper arm was missing. The thought occurred to her that this wound happened when it crashed the blackened meteor on that scorched path of earth lying back in the woods. The meteor had to be its ship.

She couldn't breathe waiting for this creature to do to her whatever it pleased—tear her to pieces, eat the flesh from her bones, or worse. Instead, it turned toward the lake and marched her into the warm waters.

It was going to drown her. She'd heard drowning was the most painful way to die. Liza began to writhe and fight its grasp, kicking at it and thrashing her upper half around wildly.

The thing put an end to her fight with one solid head-butt, mashing her already broken nose in the process as well as delivering her to a bevy of stars and dizziness. It had her submerged up to her chin in the water before she could even see straight. But she could feel something else. Something crawling over her face, like lots of little somethings.

Liza was about to scream when she felt the creature let her go. She watched as it made its way back to the shore.

Why? Why would it let her go, unless...? Unless it knew something she didn't.

She started to swim toward the side of the lake away from the shore and the alien fuck and toward the trees. Her vision blurred. Her eyes burned like she'd spent the day swimming in a chlorine pool, only worse. If it were possible to have your eyes bleed from irritation, she was certain this was that breaking point.

She continued for the lake's edge when her knees *thunked* into something hard below the surface. She fell forward, her hands growing numb, and found a shape in the water—the front of a car. Her blurry gaze travelled upward. The old muscle car was staring her in the face.

She climbed upon it and used it to help her reach her destination.

As she reached the tall bushes and small trees just on the other side, she fell to the land and shrieked. The pain in her eyes immense and paralyzing. Everything went dark. Her eyes were...*melting*.

Her screams sounded phlegmy; her tongue felt more like dissolving tissue in her mouth. She reached with her fingers and met gum and teeth. Her lips were gone.

Her mind reached its threshold for the impossible as her body went into spams.

***

On the beach, Grace's eyes fluttered open. What she saw before her sucked the air from her lungs. A blanket of thousands of glowing microbes or fungus or alien algae, whatever the fuck it was, covered the water near the rocky shore. The space monster stood at the water's edge, it's arms out, welcoming the glowing blanket inland. She watched as the shining fungus came to its master and climbed the being until it was completely engulfed, and the lake was clear and dark again.

After a few minutes, the luminance of the fungi dimmed and went out. When it was done, the space creature turned. Tremors wracked Grace's body; whether from fear of this thing or from the wound it had inflicted earlier, she didn't know.

It stood over her not making a sound.

She considered asking for mercy.

It raised its foot over her face. She closed her eye as it brought the boot down and ended her.

***

Healed and undiscovered, the alien creature snatched the dead Earthling by the hair and dragged her lifeless body into the woods. It would need to repair its craft. Until then, it would make its home by the lake. There would be plenty of nourishment.

# THE GUIDE

Declan watched the broken man make his way through the valley of homeless people. He observed this man closely, curious as the man went about actions that were like witnessing an actor on a stage. The man stepped around filthy and hungry folks, desolate and alone in their togetherness. When the man sought out an empty corner and tucked his knees to his chest, Declan waited. The man's eyes closed as he dropped his head to his knees and tried to fall asleep.

"Hey," Declan said. "Boyo."

The man raised his chin and stared. "Hi, can I help you?"

"Yeah, you can tell me your story."

The guy waved him off and lowered his head. "Sorry, man. I'm trying to get some rest."

Declan sat next to him. "Rest, eh? Well, you've got plenty of time for that. What's your name?"

"Fuck, man," the guy said, exasperated. "Go find your pot of gold somewhere else and fuck off."

"You don't know, do ya?"

"What? What are you going on about?"

Declan laughed, heartily, with his gut. He hadn't laughed since, well, since he was alive, he reckoned.

"Jesus," the guy said. "My name's Bruce, okay? Now, go bother someone else."

Declan wiped at tears that never fell and looked Bruce in the eye. "You're a ghost, boyo."

"What the hell are you on?" Bruce asked.

Declan pulled his shoulder length gray hair back in a ponytail, ran his hand over the permanent gray stubble of his face and stood. "Come with me, then."

"I told you, I need some goddamn rest."

"And I told you, you're dead. Now, get up and walk with me."

Bruce's eyes and face loosened. Declan could see his confidence waver.

"I promise ya, boyo. It's no lie. No trick. Sometimes, it happens this way. You don't even realize. Not until you try to touch someone. Try and talk to someone."

"I'm talking to you—" Bruce began, but must have caught on midway through. "You're a ghost."

Declan nodded.

He watched as Bruce looked at his own hands, touched his own face.

"But I feel..."

"Think about what you did last. When's the last time you tried to speak with someone?"

"Candy... I've called Candy, but she...she never talks to me. I thought, well, I didn't say anything the first couple times I called, but when I tried to apologize the other day, she just kept saying hello. She was crying and she said hello...then, she hung up." Bruce looked up to him. "She couldn't hear me. It wasn't the connection, it was..."

Declan nodded.

Bruce rose. "But when? How?"

"Think back a little further. Do you remember anything like someone coming at you? Maybe an accident? Take a little too much of something ya shouldn't?"

"No, I don't do drugs, man. I just...I just drink a little."

"And no one attacked ya?"

Bruce shook his head. Then his knees buckled. He stumbled to the concrete wall.

"What is it?" Declan asked.

"I left them."

"Who?"

"My wife...Candy. My, my boy...Harlan."

"Go on."

"I couldn't take it. I've been out of work for almost six months. Got laid off from Brigham Steel, forced to crawl to the unemployment office. I had to face them with nothing. I was becoming an anchor. Candy busted her ass at the diner in the night and cleaning houses in the day. And I just...I just kept drinking."

"Sounds like hard times," Declan said.

"Yeah," he sighed.

"That night...it was raining, and the river was threatening to swell. I got up, patted Harlan on the head while he watched his cartoon. I told Candy I was going out...out to...hell, I don't remember."

"It's okay, boyo. Go on."

Declan played witness as the man fell apart on the inside. Bruce brought his hands up to his eyes as his body shook. It was something awful to watch a man come undone like this, but it was part of the process.

When he had himself under control, Bruce wiped at non-existent tears and continued. "I got in my truck, cracked a beer, then just drove. I drove until my eyes were blurry, and I remember wishing to God to just take me with the storm, to just drown me already and be done with it. And that's when...I drifted...I let go. I let go of the wheel and the truck hydroplaned."

Bruce collapsed back to the spot he'd settled in before to rest.

"The headlights of another truck coming the other way were suddenly shining on me from the left. I turned to them and I thought of God's eyes..." Bruce looked up and then to Declan. "Is that it? Was that when I died?"

Declan reached a hand to him.

"How come I could call her?" he asked.

"We can't contact the living. Can't speak to them, touch them. But inanimate objects or," he nodded for Bruce to take his hand.

Bruce reached up and grasped his hand and allowed Declan to help him to his feet.

"We can connect with others who have passed. We can move objects. How do you think Poltergeists and all that haunting shite happens?"

Bruce looked to him with eagerness in his eyes. "Can we go see them?"

"Ah, now that's a hard road."

"Please? Will you go with me?"

"You wanna talk about pain, boyo? You think standing here with me, talking about it is hard? You stand before your loved ones...and you'll know devastation."

"I don't care. I can handle it, and if I can't, well..."

"Hmm, yeah, well, then I'll be there for ya. Come on then."

They walked. Declan headed straight for people, Bruce reaching out to pull him aside until he passed right through them. When they reached a busier part of town, Declan walked right into the street and laughed as Bruce dodged and ducked from vehicles until a city bus caught him head on.

Giddiness rolled through the man.

"It ain't all that bad," Declan said.

They continued. Time and distance were irrelevant. They talked about how to spend the days, the nights...Bruce asked how long Declan had been a ghost. How long would they be here? Was there a Heaven.

Declan explained that he'd drank himself to death after the loss of his wife, Helena. Could have been five years ago, could have been much longer. He'd only lost track of one other ghost, a girl named Misty. She followed him around a while until one day she was gone. If Heaven existed, he was sure she was there.

They came upon a small bungalow, faded blue with flaking white shudders.

"This is it?" Declan asked.

"Yeah," he said.

"Well, go have yourself a look."

"Will you...come with me?"

"Ay, if you want me to."

They walked to window just left of the front steps.

And there they were. And they were in tears.

"No..." Bruce whispered; his voice trembled.

The boy, Harlan, was in his mother's arms. She was rocking him on the edge of the sofa.

Bruce headed for the door and was out of reach as Declan tried to stop him. Instead, he followed the man inside the house. They stopped at the edge of the living room.

A piece of paper lay at Candy's feet. Declan could see it was a drawing done in crayon. Wet with teardrops, it featured two figures—one big, one small. And three heartbreaking words: Love you Daddy.

Bruce dropped to his knees and sobbed. Candy and Harlan looked past them both, toward the door. Neither moved.

Declan knelt beside Bruce and put his arms around him. "I tried to warn ya, boyo."

He felt his own sorrow come back from the dead as he held the man.

"Hello?" Candy sat Harlan aside and walked past the two ghosts in her living room. She came back into the room and said, "It must have been the wind."

"Do you think we'll see him again?" Harlan asked, his big brown eyes staring into his mothers.

"I'm sure he's watching over us, baby."

***

Declan stood on the sidewalk watching the living room window.

"You're gonna stay with them, ain't ya, boyo?"

"Yes. It hurts, but...I'll stay with them as long as I can. Seeing them, hearing them, it's better than nothing."

"Ay," Decan patted him on the back. "You're a stronger man than you thought, eh?"

"I guess I am."

"Watch over that there boy of yours. If you need me, I'll be around. Until I'm not, I guess."

"Declan," Bruce called out.

He turned and looked back.

"Thank you."

He nodded.

That's how it happened sometimes. Declan wasn't an official guide. He'd never been anointed as such by God or whatever presence was up there controlling it all. It just seemed that he had a knack for finding these new ghosts and helping them. And he had to admit, it brought a warmth that had otherwise died out long ago.

Smiling in the rain, a fresh warmth inside him, Declan walked down the road toward his next lost soul.

# EVERETT

Bret bought her the doll for comfort. Ever since Arnold's death, Teresa's depression had morphed into something ugly and dangerous. She didn't sleep. A steady diet of cigarettes, alcohol, and Prozac fueled her will to exist. Christmas delivered more restlessness from her, but tonight he would present her with the doll—a three-foot-tall, black-haired boy doll with a white dress shirt and black dress pants. With his skinny, porcelain face, Sharpie black eyebrows and pink lips, he reminded Bret of a mini Jehovah's Witness. Teresa would love him. Bret knew it in his heart.

"I don't want any presents," she said from behind a cloud of smoke.

Bret placed the box on the kitchen table before her.

She rolled her eyes, stuck the cigarette in her mouth, and tore the blue tissue paper he'd used to wrap the doll. The face, the perfect blue glass eyes uncovered, Teresa placed her smoke in the ashtray and steepled her hands over her nose and mouth. The cigarette burned out as she gazed at the boy, *her boy*, and cried.

"Bret," she whispered. "He's beautiful."

He smiled as she gently removed the rest of the soft paper. Lifting him up with her hands cupped under his arms, she stared into those reflective eyes.

"Everett." Christened, the boy became the center of Teresa's world.

***

"Teresa, why is Everett in my chair?"

The stairs creaked as she made her way down. "He likes it. You can sit on the couch, right?"

Bret didn't like the look in her eyes. It was too gazey, too *somewhere else*.

The change in her appearance and her spirit over the last four and a half months had been uplifting, at first. She wasn't moping around in her sweats or housecoat anymore. She wasn't swimming in her vodka bottles, and she'd even quit smoking cold turkey. But when she started talking to Everett, like he was a real boy, whispering, giggling, responding to questions unheard, his stomach soured.

"I don't want him in my chair. That's my spot."

"Don't you touch him."

He was speared by the daggers in her gaze.

"Why don't you go watch your baseball game at Mark's."

Bret hated to admit it, but there was something unsettling choking the air around them. He ducked his chin to his chest and did as she suggested.

Grabbing his sweatshirt from the back of the chair, he could swear Everett's arm moved. Just a little.

*No*, he told himself. *Not possible*. But when he raised his gaze to Teresa, she smirked.

"I'll be back later," he said, trying to swallow the queasy feeling.

***

Mark's house was on Cyprus Street, a fifteen-minute drive. He lived alone following the death of his wife, Heather. The two men met at a group for people grieving lost loved ones. That had been just over a year ago. Heather had been gone three years this Christmas. Almost overnight, he and Mark had become fast friends. It was Mark who suggested getting Teresa the doll from Cayman's. Mark's mother had a ton of them, and he joked that she loved them like they were his siblings.

Bret pulled his Dodge into the driveway beside Mark's Jeep.

Mark greeted him at the door. "What's up, bro?"

They fist bumped. "T exiled me. It seems Everett has taken my place."

Mark gave him an uneven grin.

"Not really," Bret said. "She told me to watch the game over here."

"Oh," Mark said, then nodded for him to come inside.

It was the sixth inning, Mets up over the Nats 4-1. They had a few beers and a bag of tortilla chips polished off when it finally slipped: "I don't like that doll."

"Who, Everett?"

"Yes. He gives me the creeps. And it's not just him, man. T is acting all... I don't know."

"I thought you said she was doing well?"

"She was, er...she is, but it's just... I can't put my finger on it, you know?"

"Well, what's she doing that weirds you out?"

"Like this morning, I came down and the doll was in my chair. That's not that odd—annoying, but not odd. But then she comes downstairs as I'm getting ready to move him—it—and she tells me not to touch him. That's when she told me to get lost."

Mark opened another beer and sat back in his EZ chair. "I don't know, man. I think you're reading too much into it. Sounds like you're placing an underlying issue between the two of you on that doll."

Bret leaned forward with his hands knitted together. Mark was probably right. The guy seemed like a *Devil-may-care* type with his bandanas, chin beard, tattooed neck, and heavy metal band t-shirts, but he was maybe the smartest, most insightful person Bret had ever met.

"Shit, man, I know you're right. It's just..." Even still, there was something. "Ah, fuck it, man." Bret snagged another beer and focused on the game.

"Dude," Mark said. "Fuck it. Cheers!"

They clinked their bottles together and set about enjoying the rest of the game.

***

When Bret got home, he found Teresa and Everett lying on the sofa. She was in a nighty. Her eyes were wide open but unmoving.

"Holy shit," he said, hurrying before her. Just as he touched her, her gaze shifted to him. His heart hammered in his chest. "Jesus, T, I thought..."

"What? That I was dead?"

"Yeah." He turned and looked at the TV set. It was off. "What are you doing?"

"We were just lying here relaxing."

Bret reached down for the doll.

"What do you want?" she asked, her brow furrowing like a storm above her oily eyes.

"We need to talk."

She sat up and pulled Everett close.

"Can we just set the doll aside for a minute?" he asked.

"Why? He's a doll, Bret. He's not going to hear all your dark secrets." Again, that odd knowing smirk formed on her face.

"Fine, whatever," he said, sitting down upon the coffee table. "Forget about the doll—"

"Everett," she said.

"Yeah, Everett, whatever. How have you been feeling about us?"

"Us?"

"Yeah, I mean, since I got you the doll—sorry, Everett—you've been a lot happier, right?"

"Yes. I love him. He's made all the hurt go away," she said stroking the doll's leg.

"Right," he said, trying to brush her comment aside. "Are *we* still okay?"

"Oh my God, Bret, are you jealous of Everett? Is that what this is about?"

"What? No, I'm talking about *us. Our* relationship."

Now she was grinning like the Cheshire fucking cat. "Oh, Bret." Her eyes looked him over. "Do you need some attention?"

"Well, kind of, yeah. That would be nice for a change."

She picked Everett up and looked the doll in the eyes. "I'm going to go upstairs with Bret for a little bit, okay? I'll be back."

She got up and set the doll in the recliner, and then turned to Bret. "Come with me."

He took her hand and followed her up to their bedroom. They made love for the first time in months. It was fantastic.

*****

Bret awoke in the dark. Reaching for Teresa, he found the bed empty. The red LED lights of the alarm clock read: 1:49.

He slid his feet out from under the covers and found his underwear where he'd tossed them on the bedroom floor.

There wasn't a light on in the house.

He checked the upstairs bathroom, but it was empty. Stopping at the top of the stairs, he couldn't see her on the sofa. He made his way downstairs.

The doll was no longer in his chair.

The kitchen and back bedroom they used as a computer room were also empty.

He was standing at the kitchen counter wondering where the fuck his wife could be when he heard moaning come from the door to the garage.

*What the fuck?*

Creeping across the floor, Bret placed his ear to the door and heard it again. He knew that sound; he knew all of Teresa's sounds. She'd just made these noises a few hours ago upstairs with him.

He gripped the doorknob and prepared himself for the possibility that his wife was fucking another man. But who? Who the hell had she met? When the hell had she been out? Teresa could have met some jagoff online. She had all day to talk with anyone.

He turned the knob and shoved the door open.

"Jesus, Bret," she said, startled and standing just on the other side of the door holding a lit candle in one hand with Everett tucked safely under her other arm. "You scared the shit out of me."

He looked over her shoulder. The garage was dark. Pushing past her, he searched for whoever else was out here.

"What are you doing?" she asked.

There was no one here. Both cars were outside in the driveway. Both garage doors were closed. He would have heard them open if someone had sneaked out.

"Bret?"

"I thought..."

What the hell had he thought?

*That my wife was just out here fucking someone else.*

"I don't know. I woke up and you were gone, and you weren't downstairs..."

"Well, I'm fine, and you're freaking me out. Come back inside."

In a daze, Bret walked inside. Teresa followed and closed the door behind them.

"What were you doing out there?" he asked.

She walked through the kitchen, stopping at the stairs. "I couldn't sleep, so I came down here. I thought I heard something in the garage, so I went out to look."

"With a candle and your d— Everett?"

"I didn't want to wake you by turning on all the lights, and even though I was sure it was nothing, bringing Everett made me feel better."

"But..."

*What about the moaning?*

He couldn't bring himself to say it out loud.

"But what?" she asked. He could swear she was grinning again.

"Nothing, I guess. Let's go back to bed."

***

He had work the next day. Even at the Books A Million bookstore, where he was the manager, he couldn't stop hearing Teresa behind that garage door. It was making him crazy. He considered calling Mark about it, but the last thing he needed was for his friend to confirm that he was losing his shit.

He finished the day and stopped at his favorite pub, *Harry's Place*. Mark was drinking at the end of the bar.

"What's up?" he asked. "You look like something's eating you, man."

Bret ordered a beer. "Nothing, man. Hard day at work."

"You sure? Did you and Teresa talk last night?"

He nodded as his beer arrived. "Thanks, Mel," he said to the young bartender.

"And?"

"We talked briefly, then we fucked, and I passed out."

"You sly dog." He punched Bret in the shoulder and raised his glass. "Cheers to that!"

"It was good, but…"

"Oh no, don't," Mark said. "Don't add a *but*. Just accept the little things, man."

"It just…it was nice…but it was like she used sex to shush me, you know?"

"Dude," Mark said. "You gotta learn to take the good and enjoy it. You guys are in the middle of this thing. This relationship hardship if you will. It ain't something that's just going to magically repair itself overnight. Baby steps, bro. Baby steps. Don't you remember *What About Bob?*"

"Really? You're giving me life advice from a Bill Murray movie?"

"Yes. That's exactly what I'm doing."

"Maybe you're right."

"Dude, I'm always right."

***

When he got home, buzzed from his beer and two Long Island Iced teas, he parked his car next to Teresa's and lifted the garage door. The room was sparse. They'd never collected much in the way of junk. Neither he nor Teresa were sentimental types. They weren't quite minimalists either, but they just didn't hang on to things like other friends they knew. The back wall held his modest number of tools and an old boombox he'd got from the side of the road someone was tossing out. There was a stack of books they'd received from one of the early group meetings from the grief counselors. Bret couldn't bring himself to look through them yet, but he knew, when he was ready, he'd find something helpful within at least one of them. The lawn tools, a rake, the mower, a wheelbarrow, some gardening items they'd yet to use, were all lined up against the wall to his right. To his left, their bikes.

What was missing was any and all signs of Arnold. They'd agreed the best way to move forward was to give all the baby stuff and toddler toys to Goodwill. Their keepsakes for their son were in a cardboard box up in the back of their bedroom closet.

Thinking of his boy now, brought tears to his eyes.

Inside, he could hear Teresa singing upstairs. He turned on the TV and saw Everett sitting in his chair.

"Screw you." He picked the doll up by its black hair and tossed it to the couch. Bret plopped down in his seat and caught the end of the evening news.

"Did you touch him?" Teresa's voice was sharp, venomous.

"What?"

"I told you not to touch him," she said.

"Nice to see you too, T."

She stomped down the stairs, pausing at his feet, and slapped him hard across the face.

"Jesus, T, what the fuck is wrong with you?" he said rubbing the hot flesh of his cheek.

"If you ruined him, I swear I'll make you pay."

"What the hell are you talking about?"

Teresa went to the doll, cradled it in her arms, then hurried upstairs. She didn't come down again.

***

At some point in the night, Bret fell asleep in his chair. When he woke up, an infomercial was playing, and the rest of the house was dead silent.

Recalling Teresa's fit earlier, he touched his cheek and felt the phantom strike. On his feet, Bret started for the downstairs bathroom when he heard it again. The moaning. It was coming from directly above him, in their bedroom.

Rage slithered through his veins, coiling tightly around his core as he went to the hall closet in search of a weapon. Whoever was up there with his wife was going to fucking wish he wasn't. The shelf before him held a couple of screwdrivers, a roll of duct tape, and a hammer. He picked the hammer and crept his way up the stairs. This time, he would catch this motherfucker in the goddamn act.

His imagination tortured him with the sight of T with her legs up in the air and some hound dog piece of shit thrusting into her. Their sweat-drenched bodies glistening as skin slapped skin. A tendril of hurt writhed inside him. He chose to bite down hard on the anger and let it carry him.

The sound of her ecstasy on the other side of the bedroom door buckled his knees and sent him into a fury. He didn't even bother trying the knob. Hatred and betrayal overcame his sorrow as he kicked the barrier, breaking the latch and sending the door wide open.

He was unprepared for what he witnessed.

Everett lay on the carpeted floor beneath Teresa. She was naked and sweaty, just as he imagined, only there was no man in here with her. She jumped from the doll and covered herself with the comforter from their bed. Everett lay prone, an inappropriate and impossible cock or dildo, or something Bret wanted instantly erased from his mind, stood erect from the doll's crotch.

"Get out!" Teresa screamed; her voice came out in a quiver.

He was speechless.

"Damn it, I said get out. Leave us alone."

A thousand shades of wrong and disgust moved in a chunky river of confusion and pain through him. He gazed at his wife. There was no shame in her eyes. When he looked back at the doll, its phallic obscenity was gone.

Had he really seen it?

He stepped into the room, clutching the hammer.

"What are you doing?" Teresa asked. "Bret? Don't touch him."

"Shut up. Just shut the fuck up," he cried.

He knelt beside the doll he'd caught his wife fucking and grabbed it by the front of its pristine white dress shirt.

"Bret, no!"

He raised the hammer and brought it down on the doll's face. A chunk of its shiny glass eye broke off.

Teresa cried out as if he'd struck her.

Bret reared back and delivered a second and third blow, obliterating Everett's other eye and caving in the dolls face. He was readying for a fourth blow when Teresa growled from the bed and tackled him.

The hammer dropped to the floor as they rolled together, each trying to control the other. They came to a stop as they hit the door to the walk-in closet.

"Get a hold of yourself," he shouted.

"You ruined everything!"

He tried his best to restrain her, but she was slick with sweat and managed to pull an arm free. He caught her tiny but ferocious bony fist right in the eye. She landed another shot to the same spot before catching him with a knee in his balls. Instead of getting off of him, Teresa pinned his wrists to the ground with her knees. Her sex nearly at his chin.

"What the hell, T? What is this?"

Her anger seemed to evaporate before his eyes as a smile spread across her features. She was no longer looking at him, but instead, her attention turned toward the bed, back toward Everett.

"Yes," she said, nodding in that direction. "Do it."

"Do what?" Bret said.

He craned his neck in time to see the doll upright and holding the hammer. Its head reformed and like brand-new. Bret fought to break free of his wife's grasp when the hammer dropped and cracked his skull.

***

He could see Mark as he entered the hospital room with a gym bag on his shoulder. Bret didn't know how long he'd been in a coma, but it was more than a few weeks. He'd awoken unable to move his legs, and his arms trembled of their own volition. He'd heard the doctors tell Teresa that he'd suffered severe head trauma, but that there was a good chance he'd walk and talk again.

Bret tried to recall the accident—surely it had been an accident. His memory was a foggy maze he couldn't navigate.

Teresa had spent a few hours the last couple of days reading at his bedside. She'd petted his arm and smiled from time to time, but she didn't waste her breath on him. She'd spoken with nurses and the doctors and that was it.

Why wouldn't she talk to him?

As it was, he felt trapped in his body. Stuck in some kind of nightmare. At least he had his sight and hearing.

He watched as Mark spoke with a nurse. They laughed.

"Hey, man," he said as the nurse made her way out of the room. "Teresa told me you couldn't speak, so I'll just say a few words and let you rest. I'm sorry I sent you to Cayman. I never should have done that, but after what you told me about T and how she was suffering with Arnold's death, I thought he'd help."

Bret tried to remember. He had no idea what Mark was talking about. Who was Cayman? And what had Bret said about Teresa and Arnold?

"Cayman just helps give them life. He can't control them or know how they will be once they become animated."

*Animated?*

Mark opened the gym bag strapped to his shoulder. He pulled out a doll. Blonde hair, crystal blue glass eyes. This doll had breasts beneath its black Venom t-shirt.

Who would put breasts on a doll?

The thought passed.

"This is Gina. Cayman thought she'd help me get through the days and nights without Heather. My wife was taken from me, and I miss her, but Gina here..." Mark gazed lovingly at the doll and touched her life-like lips with his thumb. "Gina makes it easier, you know? I'm even *happy* now."

In his mind, Bret suddenly saw the doll...Teresa's doll.

"I knew Everett would help Teresa," Mark said. "I'm truly sorry it came to this."

Did Mark know more about Everett? Who was Cayman?

"I thought he'd be a replacement for Arnold, but Cayman says that's not up to him. Each doll has their own set of rules and personalities."

Bret wanted to scream. He wanted to ask his friend what the hell this was all about.

"Looks like Everett decided to replace you instead, old buddy."

He tucked the doll he called Gina back into his bag and looked around the room, even ducking his head out the door as if he was looking for someone.

*...or to see if anyone is coming.*

He came back inside and slowly closed the door to the room. Mark reached into the bag again and this time produced a syringe. "We can't have you coming back and telling anyone about Cayman or his gifts."

Bret tried to move, tried to scream, tried to plead with his friend with his eyes. His hands trembled as tears spilled down the sides of his temples.

"I thought she could do it, but she didn't want to be stuck with the memory of killing you." Mark stabbed the needle into the side of Bret's neck. "Sorry, bro. Fuck it, right?"

A coldness spread from his neck to his chest.

Bret took one last breath as he saw Mark stuff the needle in his bag and hurry out the door. Within seconds, his eyes glassed over, leaving him staring at the ceiling.

A final name crossed his failing mind: *Everett*.

# You Can Have It All Back

She had begun to hear a voice. Not aloud, not from under her bed, or from the back corner of her bedroom closet, but from within. At first, Kyra thought it was just her negative thoughts manifesting into the voice of her constant pain that came with her terminal diagnosis. The whispers began in those times of weakness, when she would close her eyes and do the thing she feared most—fall asleep. She dreaded losing out on any of her remaining moments, limited and worthless as they may be, under the Sandman's dark wings.

As the days and nights passed, the voice grew clearer, making offers from the corners of her dreams. Dreams of her old life, dreams of surfing, tanning, and strutting along the beaches of Southern California. The boys of summer, blond and bronzed, ripe with promise of one-night stands, ogling her as she soaked in the sun, grinning from ear to ear, biting her lip, and driving them all absolutely mad.

It was in these dreams where she began to see the faceless little boy. Was it his voice? As sleep gripped her, pulling her under despite her protests, the medicine too much for her weakened state, she found herself searching for *him*. The beach hunks became stock-art, fading into the scene, while the boy was always there, just out of reach, silent and still, standing at the ocean's edge, the waves creeping to his heels.

Kyra felt the cancer inside her hammering its coffin nails. She could no longer move without assistance. Her ability to speak reduced to marble mouthed nonsense. She was beyond devastation, wandering her withered mind without a care for anything but the boy—the alluring, faceless enigma beckoning from her dreams. It was here that desperation welcomed her with open arms.

She now dreamt while awake and had begun to see the boy in the corner of her room.

Her hospice nurse, Clayton, had been with her for the last ten days. Along with cleaning up her accidents and making sure she got her pain meds in a timely fashion, it seemed he felt compelled to spout his fantastical rhetoric of a paradise in the sky, and of a God of forgiveness and love. She tried to tell him to kindly shut the fuck up, but her words came out broken and unintelligible.

God was a fairy tale for the feeble minded. In the faceless boy, she had found a mystical force that she could *see*. Today, for the first time, she heard his message with perfect clarity.

*Pass it on and you can have it all back.*

She awoke, slick with sickness purging from her pores. Her eyes flittered open as she watched the shore of her dreams fade into the pale blue wall of her death room. The phantom scent of sunblock wafted past her like an apparition as she saw the faceless boy in the corner again.

Clayton sat in the chair next to her bed, fast asleep with his hands folded over a paperback in his lap, a smile touching the corners of his blubbery lips.

*Pass it on and you can have it all back.*

"Haa?" she asked aloud. "Teh m-me haa..."

*I'll show you.*

Her arms lifted of their own volition. She watched, amazed; excitement surged through her prickling mind. Kyra should have been frightened, but instead, she smiled, genuinely smiled for the first time in months. She was a tattered marionette eager to see what happened next. It was wrong. Kyra knew it in her heart but couldn't bring herself to care. A new strength surged in her bones, in her blood, in her soul. Sitting up, her feet slid from beneath the covers and plopped to the floor between the bed and Clayton's chair. Alive again, she watched her hands wrap around the aging flesh of the nurse's throat.

"Kyra?" Clayton wheezed beneath her grip. The man squirmed, trying to break free but could not.

She lifted her gaze from Clayton's tear-filled, petrified eyes and found the faceless boy standing inches from her. And with one blackened finger, he pointed to Clayton's gaping mouth as the struggling caregiver gasped for breath.

*Pass it on.*

Kyra saw image after image flash before her eyes. Images of herself suffering the effects of the chemo— her pallid flesh, her withering body, her emptying stomach—and she understood.

"Pass it on," she spoke aloud, giddy at hearing her voice, clear and true. The boy or spirit or whatever he was, he was doing this. He was marvelous. "Pass it on and I can have it all back."

Clayton gazed to the bedside, confusion in his eyes. "Ky...ra, wh-what are you t-talking about?"

Her bony fist swung down like a ball-peen hammer, crunching Clayton's nose. Blood exploded over his mouth and chin. This time, instead of choking him, Kyra hands clenched the sides of his head and held his face still.

Clayton screamed.

"Perfect," she said.

Before he could grasp her intentions, the black plague that had been devouring her insides, robbing her of her voice, her strength, her beauty, her life, spewed forward in a rush of hot, foul fluid. Clots of ruined cells and thick, wet lumps of deteriorating organs rained out from her mouth passing into the caregiver's.

*Pass it on and you can have it all back.*

***

Four days later, Kyra Adams lay under the sun on Huntington Beach, a frosty beverage in hand and a permanent grin upon her face. Her body, fully recovered and filling out the brand-new purple two-piece she'd picked up this morning, soaked in the warmth as she watched the summertime boys passing by with their bronzed pecs and abs on full display.

Though she had looked for him, she had not seen the faceless boy since that day in her death room.

Clayton Shaw had come with her to California. She couldn't exactly leave the man at her home in his new condition. The caregiver was chained to the toilet in the beach house she'd rented. He was in a bad way, fading fast, much faster than she had been. He would be dead by the end of the week.

Tossing the beer aside, she stood and winked at one of her bronzed admirers. She was ready for the waves and happy to be back to the good life.

# MOURNING PICTURES

My sister used to send me the best pictures—dogs shitting on pristinely-manicured lawns, random porta-potties with crumpled Doritos bags or discarded Skoal containers by the door, shitty old Monte Carlos purposely taking up two spots to avoid scratches. She even had a professional looking logo on the bottom right corner of every shot: Veronica Johnson Photography. When she died last year, these daily reminders, these morning pictures she sent me, were one of the things I missed most. I saved and curated them all in a folder titled "Mourning Pictures" on my laptop. I told our mom I was going to have a proper coffee table book made of Roni's pictures, but Mom thought the shots were in poor taste. I argued otherwise.

It truly was art. My sister may not have recognized the potential—hell, maybe she did—but I saw it the first time she sent me a picture of a sign that said: **Please, No Photography.** I laughed so hard coffee shot out my nose. The coffee table book idea came from an episode of *Seinfeld* Roni and I had watched together, over and over again. I wanted to make this one small project happen. I wanted to pay tribute to her, even if the finished product resided only with me.

I decided this morning I was ready to open the folder on my computer. I held the cursor over it for a good two minutes. Emotions hit me in waves. There was a tsunami of sadness and joy in this one click. They'd all be there, all three hundred plus shots, everything from the picture of the poodle and the bull mastiff shitting side by side to the hotel toilet with a corded phone just above the tank.

Still, I hesitated.

I moved the curser to the next folder over. These were pictures of us. Without thinking, I gave the mouse a double-tap and watched as the shot of her and I at the Dropkick Murphys/U.S. Bombs show filled the screen. The picture was taken in 1998 at a club called The Asylum. She was 22. I had just turned 19. I was decked out in spiked green hair and a Rancid hoodie. She wore her black hair in a ponytail and looked tough as hell in her leather jacket and Metallica *Ride the Lightning* t-shirt. She wasn't into punk so much. No, my sister was a metalhead, through and through, who also harbored a sick fascination with '80s glam bands. The show was a birthday present for me.

Looking at the photo, I could see why people always thought we were twins. We both had our mother's hazel eyes and her snub nose, plus dad's straight hair and long face. We shared the same damn smile, too. This picture was from a pre-iPhone age. I believe a disposable Kodak was the instrument of choice. In the years since, I'd scanned a ton of old pictures onto my computer. This shot didn't make me as sad as I thought it might. It was a fun night, a *good* memory. Clicking through the older photos, I eventually found my way to newer ones.

I couldn't do it. My eyes welled up as I bit my lips and held the tears at bay.

Closing out of the folder, I took a deep breath before exhaling slow and steady. I knew this was going to be hard but dammit, this fucking hurt. I wanted to include some pictures of the two of us together in the coffee book project, but looking at her face, her smile—this part was just going to have to wait a while longer.

I went back to the daily photos file and clicked the mouse before I could chicken out.

Nothing.

There was nothing.

"Uh, what?"

I x'd out of the folder and tried again.

*This folder is empty.*

All those pictures...the dogs, the potty shots, the pizza slices plopped on the beautiful oak wood floors and crystalline glass tables, the ashtray chained to a lamppost that had a *Clean Air Zone* sign fastened to it. All lost.

"What the actual fuck? Where the hell are they?"

I could feel the neurons firing a fury of activity within my mind. I was suddenly a junky overcome with the cravings that made them fidget and scratch at old scabs. If her pictures were gone, *all* gone, I was going to fucking lose my shit.

I had Roni's old Ford Focus, the one she sold me for $500. I had her vinyl collection—Twisted Sister, Bon Jovi, David Lee Roth solo albums and all. I had her Patriots hoodie and winter cap embroidered with #12 (even though I was a Jets fan and loathed her love for Tom Brady). It was all perfect and meaningful, I cherished every bit of her that I still had, but the pictures...those were *ours.* Despite living hours from one another, despite her job and kids, and my work and my weed, every morning, there was the *blip* from my cell notifying me that she'd sent me her daily photo, the one thing that kept us connected as grown-ups.

And they were all fucking gone.

I exited out of the folder and ran a search on my computer. I sat there, my knees bouncing as I rubbed my hands together tweaking out as I watched the little spinning wheel on my screen—the laptop not seeking out strange new worlds but rather the pieces of my heart.

Then the screen went black.

"Now what?"

Tilting my head to the side, I could see that the cord was still attached to the outlet, but the power light next to the USB port had gone dark. I hit the power button, then held it down. It was useless. The damn thing wouldn't turn on.

Sitting back in my chair, I steepled my hands over my nose and mouth, and tried to hold it together.

My living room window was closed, yet a cool breeze lifted the hairs off my forehead and sent goose bumps crawling over my arms.

*Blip*

I gazed at the new Samsung Galaxy next to me resting atop my record player. It took me a second to realize I was holding my breath. I sat up and reached for the phone. My eyes went wide as the hairs on my forearm began to rise like a radio antenna seeking out airwaves. My breathing quickened as my arm began to shake.

The phone to my ear, the quiet hum it emitted chilled my insides.

I heard a dog whimpering and whining from behind me. I spun but nothing was there.

*Ring, ring*

An old school telephone called out from somewhere down the hall.

Jumping to my feet, I saw a green tin ashtray sitting beneath my white board in the kitchen. Scrawled in purple dry-erase marker in Roni's big, loopy script was *Clean Air Zone*.

The dog whine came again accompanied by a scratch at my door.

The loud ass phone continued to ring from down the hall. I needed to make it stop before it induced insanity. Ignoring the scratching at the door and the other impossibilities popping up in my apartment, I started toward the awful sound.

My foot slipped into something warm and mushy. Oatmeal came to mind, but as I lost my balance and fell. I hit the floor hard. My head cracked against floor bringing out the stars as all the air escaped my lungs. The scent of dog shit blasted my senses. For the briefest of seconds, the madness all faded beneath a muffled buzz. But just as quickly as it all fell away, the impossibilities roared back in an overwhelming rush of sight and sound.

I sat up, half expecting the dog shit to be gone, but there it sat smudged between my toes and across the floor where my bare foot had found it.

"Fuck!" I shouted.

I slammed my fist on the floor and stood.

The goddamn *ringing* continued.

I snagged a dish towel from the counter and did my best to wipe the shit from between my toes.

"Shut up!" I yelled at the dogs I still couldn't see. There was definitely more than one now.

Dropping the dirty rag in the trash can, and careful to step around the dog shit, I stalked down the hall and found the blaring phone coming from my bathroom. There above my toilet tank was a beige corded telephone. The room wobbled around me, the unreality of it all becoming too much.

I steadied myself by grasping the doorframe, clutching at something tangible, leaning my forehead against the solid wood for connection as I closed my eyes. The barking and scratching at the front door grew in their intensity, the phone raged on pummeling my senses.

"Roni!"

My apartment was swallowed by the silence.

Panting, seconds away from having some sort of emotional conniption fit or a fucking panic attack, I opened my eyes. The phone above my toilet was gone. Gazing down the hall, so was the pile of crap on the floor. No more barking. No more scratching.

*Blip*

Mystified, I wandered like a ghost down the hall, passing the white board that now only read *Need more beer!* scrawled in my own chicken scratch in blue marker.

As I reached my desk, I could see my computer was on and the "Mourning Pictures" file was...*open.*

The shot on the screen was of a sloppy piece of cheese pizza splattered across the pristine marble floor in the entrance lobby of the esteemed Eastland Park Hotel. I wanted to laugh but couldn't.

*Blip*

I reached for my phone.

*What if...*

It was foolish to think Roni had somehow reached across the barrier of life and death, but as my fingers touched my cell, a tingle ran through me.

I plopped down on my chair, punched in my code to unlock the screen, and stared. There were three new messages from her.

I opened the first one: *Hey, bro.*

And the next: *just letting you know that I'm*

I clicked on the last one and let out a jittery gasp. Tears streamed down my face. Roni's smile lit up the screen. The photo was from the night before her accident. We'd met up at Geno's Rock Club on Congress Street to see a Ke$ha cover band, of all things. Standing outside the front doors, she held the phone at arm's length as she took this selfie of us.

On the marquee centered just above our heads was the name of the band—

*Thinking of You.*

Impossibly, down in the bottom right-hand corner of the photo was her logo...Veronica Johnson Photography.

# MASTER OF BEYOND

**T**HUSRDAY 2:55 A.M.

The sight of the Ouija board spilled a trail of spiders down Jillian's back. She wanted to tell Sean to put it back, to forget about this, but Cindy and Coop looked so damned excited, she kept her thoughts to herself.

"Yes," Coop said. "Let's talk to Satan!"

"Our luck we'll just get Jeff," Sean replied as he pulled out the board and planchette.

"Who?" Cindy asked.

"Our first maintenance guy. He was a grouchy old bastard," Coop told her.

"Cindy," Jillian said. "How could you forget? Remember, he used to tell you to call him Thunderlips?"

Cindy and Sean cracked up. Jillian used the light moment to scooch closer to Coop. He smelled amazing.

*Don't get any ideas*, she reminded herself. Cooper Murray was pure, unadulterated trouble. She'd already made the mistake of making out with him on New Year's Eve. Still, she hated messing with occult crap, even if it was supposed to be a toy. It felt blasphemous, not fun.

Sean set four black candles around the room: one on top of his record player to the right, one on the filing cabinet on the left side of the room, and two on the front corners of his desk. He shut off the lights and rejoined them around the board.

He looked at Jillian. "I know how hot you are for Coop, but we need to stay in our places. Move back to your corner."

Her face flooded with warmth as she did as Sean said.

"It's okay," Coop patted her knee. "I'll be right here." He reached over and gave her hand a squeeze.

Sean designated himself the medium. No one argued.

Things were going fine until Jillian, her fingers fluttering above the planchette, felt something cold wrap around knuckles and flutter up her arms.

"Oh," she whimpered, pulling her hand back.

"What is it?" Cindy asked.

"Come on, Jill," Sean whined. "Would you put your hands back on? We were just getting it going."

"No, no. I don't want to do this anymore." She climbed to her feet and hurried out the door.

As she stepped into the hall outside Sean and Coop's office, the lighting fixture above her head began to flicker and sway, casting amorphous shadows across the walls. Looking up, she nearly tripped at the top of the stairs. Her hand landed on the red fire alarm. She worried she'd set it off, but then, looking at its rough edges and chipped paint, she wondered if it even worked.

She hurried downstairs. The closed-up bar was lit only by the exit sign near the front door. Her nerves on edge, Jillian grabbed a bottle of vodka from behind the bar, took two big swigs, and pulled her keys from her purse.

Pausing at the door, she listened for their laughter upstairs, but it was silent. Somehow that seemed worse.

Jillian headed out into the night and went straight home.

***

"Jill," Coop said, "have you seen Sean this morning?"

"No, but I think I heard him moving around in his office. I figured he had some two-bit floozy in there. I've had enough of opening doors to half-naked women who have no class and even less self-respect."

Coop leaned on her desk. "God, I love you. When are we gonna sleep together?"

"Probably already did in your dreams last night." She winked at him and went back to her Rolodex. "Listen, get up there and see if he's okay. I have a few more calls to make this morning to secure Bad Obsession—"

"Whoa... Secure? I thought we already had them?"

"Don't freak on me. Jesus, they'll be here. The Sheraton on Bellevue had to close down due to that accident. I'm sure you heard about it, right?" She waited, but Coop seemed oblivious. "Well, there was a city bus. Driver had a stroke, crashed the bus into the lobby of the hotel and set the damn place on fire."

"Oh shit," he said.

"Yeah, oh shit. I've been hustling to find new accommodations pretty much since I got word of the closure, thank you very much. There's just some last-minute minutiae I need to nail down before they arrive tomorrow."

Coop stood and sighed. "Well, shit. Don't scare me like that, huh?"

He walked around the desk and leaned toward her cheek.

"Don't even think about it, Coop. Not after last time."

He straightened up and smirked. "Look, I thought we were past that?"

"Hmm..."

He raised his hands in surrender. "Okay, okay... Peace, all right? By the way, you missed out last night."

She didn't want to hear about that damned Ouija board. The creepiness stuck to her last night and followed her into her dreams.

"That's okay, Coop. I don't need a recap. I'm sure you guys had a good laugh at me running off like that."

"We made contact."

The words froze her veins.

***

Coop got a kick out of Jillian's nervousness over the board. Hell, he'd been a little creeped out himself when something that called itself Eiddam said, "Hello." At first, he was certain it was Sean, but when the candle flames wavered and then suddenly blew out, they all shrieked before cracking up in the dark.

It was black at the top of the stairs. When the light bulb crunched under his boots, he laughed. Maybe it was old Jeff's spirit in here last night, breaking shit so they'd still need him.

When Coop opened the door to find his partner sitting in his chair, hands folded on the desk, staring straight ahead with glowing white eyes, he nearly stumbled back into the hall. Unfortunately, his body moved into the room involuntarily, and the door slammed shut behind him.

***

Jillian hated that she still wanted to be with Cooper, but she'd be damned if she'd make the same mistake twice. It's why she was so good at her job—she needed to focus on work to *not* think about Coop. His dastardly good looks and charm made him the quintessential "heartbreaker." Pat Benatar had definitely made his acquaintance at some point.

After locking down the Bad Obsession contracts, getting the hotel arrangements set for the band, crew, and that of the MTV crew, Jillian called the office to tell the boys the good news.

"Just thought I'd let you guys know we're all good for tomorrow." She waited. "What? No applause? No, 'Hell yes?'"

They remained silent.

She hated when they put her on speaker. "Hello?'

"That's perfect," Sean said. "Could you come up here for a minute? We have something we'd like to discuss with you."

He sounded strange. His voice...like he was trying on an accent she couldn't place.

"Ah, actually I'm on lunch now. I'll check in when I get back. Are you okay, Sean?"

"Yes, that will be fine."

"Um, okay," she said. "See you boys in an hour."

She didn't wait for a response.

***

At the bar, she couldn't shake the feeling that something was wrong with Sean. When Cindy arrived, she decided to get her thoughts on the matter.

"Am I crazy?"

Cindy tossed back her margarita, put her glass down, and said, "Well, sounds like Sean's hungover. What's new? Maybe he's nervous about tomorrow. I know I would be."

"Yeah, you're probably right, but he...he just sounded like someone else."

"What about Coop?"

"He didn't say anything."

"Coop? Silent? That's a first."

"I know," she said.

She thanked the tall red headed waitress for her beer and took a sip. Twisted Sister played from the speakers as Jillian fell silent.

"Coop mentioned that you guys met Egor or something last night," Jillian said.

Cindy bit her lip, her gaze cast down at the cross pendant on her necklace.

"What? Was it really that freaky?"

"I..." Cindy started. "No...it was just Sean and Coop fucking around. You're lucky you left. They had a blast at my expense, dumb shits."

"Assholes," Jillian said.

"Well, hey, if you still feel weird about Sean and Coop just head home. You said you secured everything for tomorrow's show, right?"

"Yeah."

"Well, then fuck it. They fuck off all day and night, screwing whoever they want, snorting whatever they want. You're clean as a whistle and do most of the damn work here. The Shantyman is packed again because of you. You do your job and do it fucking well. See what's up and call it an early day so we can have a late night." Cindy smiled.

"I think I will." Jillian held her drink up. "Cheers!"

"That's the fucking spirit."

They clanged their glasses.

"To tomorrow," Jillian said.

"To rock n' roll and the future success of The Shantyman...thanks to you!"

***

"Sorry, friend, but some of us just aren't cut out for this kind of power," the demon in possession of Sean Reilly spoke.

"Sean, what's wrong with you? Your eyes..."

Coop's spine stiffened as his feet left the ground. His broad shoulders drew back, pulled by an unseen force, stretching his skin, muscle, and tendons to the point of breaking. He screamed.

"What is this?"

"You are not necessary," the demon known as Eiddam said.

The white light from his eyes blazed within the office causing the blind and pathetic fool before him to cry out.

Eiddam watched with pleasure. The human's arms ripped free of his body and thumped to the floor. Obscene and intoxicating, Eiddam sucked in the blood, pain, and torment—an airborne pathogen. Perfection.

The human's wails reached their crescendo and then ceased; the sound of ruined flesh hitting the floor in a torrent of wet thuds was a symphonic masterpiece.

When the woman, this...Jillian, returned, she would accept his gift or suffer the same consequence.

In the rooms below, they gathered, ingesting spirits and carrying on, quenching appetite's that would make Dionysus proud, but Eiddam would not reveal himself tonight. The show was to be the Master's *coup de grâce*. Earth would meet its future. Blood would fill the streets, and the Master's army would relish humanity's defeat.

When the girl never bothered to come back, Eiddam sealed the door and slumbered. He would need the rest for tomorrow's grand event.

**FRIDAY**

Jillian arrived at The Shantyman just before eleven in the morning. Luckily, she'd stuck to beer last night. Her hangover was minimal. As expected, Sean and Coop were nowhere to be found, but she was too preoccupied directing various lighting guys and managers to worry about either of them. Cindy was right. She was the reason the club functioned at a level of professionalism unmatched by any of its local competition. And as much as Sean and Coop liked to screw around, they always came through when it mattered most. They'd be here. Until then, she would be in charge.

Bad Obsession arrived promptly at five. The MTV crew, shortly after.

Jillian had everyone set up and ready to roll by 6:30 p.m. Headbanger's Ball would shoot the band's act and cut and clip the performance for tomorrow's broadcast as they saw fit.

The line of people waiting to get in wrapped around the block. This was the biggest night in The Shantyman's history.

*Where the fuck are they?*

"There you are," Cindy said, pushing past a group of big-haired blond dudes that eye-fucked her as she stepped past. "Excuse me, fellas." She smiled and ignored their come-ons.

"Got a place we can have a smoke and actually fucking hear each other?" Cindy asked.

"My office. Come on," Jillian said. "Mark?" she yelled to Mark Remme, one of their assistant managers and lead light engineer.

"Yeah?"

"I'm taking five before we get this party started. I'll be in my office if you need me, 'kay?"

"Sure thing, Jill. Have you seen or heard from Sean or Coop yet?"

"No, but they'll be here. Did you try upstairs?"

"Yeah, the door's been locked all day. I tried my key and it didn't work. They must have changed out the lock."

A hot little brunette in a leather mini skirt and leopard-print halter top handed Mark a beer. He smirked, accepting the pint, looked back to Jill and shrugged.

Jillian winked and waved as she grabbed Cindy's hand and led her through the growing throng to her back office. "Dancing on Glass" followed them down.

"Oh my God!" Cindy squealed. "New Crüe!"

She was the biggest slut for the boys in Mötley. She claimed to have fucked bassist Nikki Sixx while doing lines with the band last Christmas at some recording studio in Canoga Park.

"This is my record!" Cindy shook her ass all way down the hall and into Jillian's office. "Care if I do a couple lines?" She reached for her purse.

Jillian pulled out a pack of Camel Lights and handed one to her. Cindy took the cigarette, set it on the desk and went for the blow again.

"Cindy, come on," Jillian said, lighting her smoke and then Cindy's. "I need you for a few minutes."

"Oh, all right," she said. "The night is young." She smiled and took a puff. "So, where the fuck are Sean and Coop?"

"I told you, they've been M.I.A. all day. I've been too busy making all this happen to chase them down." Jillian sat behind her desk, and put her Minnie Mouse ashtray where they could both use it. Flicking the ash, she continued, "I called upstairs twice, called them each at home at least five times apiece. Nothing."

"Odd. Where do you think they are?"

She was about to answer when the phone rang, startling them both. "Hello?"

"I missed you last night."

She set her cigarette in the ashtray and covered the phone with her hand. "It's Sean," she whispered. "I was tired. I had an early start today, so I went home."

"Come to my office."

She hated the sound of his voice. What the hell was up with that accent?

"Sean, is Coop up there with you?"

"In a manner of speaking," he said.

"The show starts in..." She looked at her watch. "Thirty minutes. You guys might want to come down."

"I'm afraid I cannot. I'm not feeling quite myself. You'll be in charge tonight, but I'll need to see you first."

"Ah, yeah, okay. I'll...be right up."

"Splendid." He hung up.

"What?" Cindy said.

"I don't fucking know." She lit another cigarette. "He's being really fucking weird. He said he doesn't feel well or some shit. Told me I'm in charge tonight. And Coop is up there, too, I guess."

"Whoa, you think it's like a test?"

"I kind of thought so, for a minute, but something feels off." She stood. "He wants to see me before the show starts. You're coming with me."

"Now, you're weirding me out," Cindy said.

***

Jillian led the way up the stairs. It was dark as hell. She tried flicking the switch, but it did nothing. As they got closer to the top step, she noticed the broken light fixture.

"What is it?" Cindy said.

"The light fixture. It's busted out. That's why it's so fucking dark up here."

"I don't like this," Cindy said, now clasping Jillian's hand.

Something crunched beneath Jill's sneakers as she crossed beneath the broken light. "Found it." She kicked the broken bulb and pieces of the old fixture to the side. She stopped outside Sean's office and knocked.

There was no answer.

"Come on," Jill said.

"He told you to come up. Just open it," Cindy said.

Jill turned the knob, and gently shoved the door. When it opened, Sean was sitting behind his desk, surrounded by candles. She flicked the light switch on the wall just inside the door, but the darkness remained.

"I've been waiting for you," Sean said.

Again, with that fucked-up accent.

"*You've* been waiting for *me*?" Now, she was pissed. She walked straight to his desk. "Sean, do you realize what the fuck is about to happen downstairs?"

"And you brought a friend," he said.

"It's just Cindy."

"I can wait outside, really, it's no problem," Cindy said.

He folded his hands over his stomach and leaned back. "Just what I was thinking."

"I'll be right here if you need me," she said before ducking outside.

"Sean, MTV is down there. We—The Shantyman—are about to be broadcast across the fucking country. I don't even know what to say." Jillian stepped to the desk, trying to hold her tongue as she wondered what the hell he was thinking? "Have you been up here this whole time?"

"I've been here much longer than that." He rose to his feet so quick it startled her.

"Wh-where is Coop?" she said, taking a step back.

The door behind her slammed shut, and she turned at the sound.

"Coop?" Sean said. "He was torn from limb to limb until there was nothing left but pulp and human waste."

Before Jillian could move, her feet were off the ground. She shrieked as her body went prone, suspended in mid-air.

"You humans make the most delicious sounds."

***

Hearing Jillian's keening wail through the wall of sound from the club downstairs raised every fine hair on Cindy's body. She stood outside the door, the broken bulb above left her dressed in darkness.

She knocked before placing her ear to the door. "Jill? Is everything all right?" She couldn't hear anything else over the music. She pounded on the door with the underside of her hand. "Jill? Jillian? Can you hear me?"

She tried the knob and cried out as she pulled her hand away. It was red hot and now burning brightly, illuminating the gloomy space around her in a crimson glow.

*Oh shit.*

She thought of the damned Ouija board. That thing that spoke to them. *Eiddam.* What had they done?

Cindy turned and ran for the stairs, taking them two at a time, nearly falling twice as she made her way to the hall and toward the stage area. She needed to find Mark.

***

Jillian heard the pounding on the door. She knew it was Cindy trying to get back in, but she couldn't move. Her body floated over the wide desk. The candles below slid to the four corners, the flames flared around her as Sean's papers and magazines scattered to the floor.

"What are you? What do you want?" she whimpered, her back landing upon the desk.

The thing drank her in as the dancing fire flickered in Sean's eyes. His clothes split down the center of his body, as if sliced by some unseen force, and slipped to the floor. His exposed flesh bubbled, oozing mucus.

Jillian's stomach turned like curdled milk.

"I am the one called Eiddam. I serve my master, and he has waited more than a century to return to this place."

"This place?"

"There are many points around this wretched world, places of complete evil, where the veil has been thinned by the wickedness of mankind and the monsters on the other side."

He stepped toward her, blackened nails split forth from the ends of his fingers. Swiping a tear from her cheek, he brought the salty discharge to the snake-like tongue darting from his lips. "How wonderful," he said, sucking at the wetness. His body shuddered. "Now, I'm going to give you an opportunity your companions were not extended."

"No..." she whispered as he reached for her. "Please...no... I'll do whatever you want."

"Yes. You will, won't you?" Eiddam said.

He reached down, touching a nail to her flesh, applying just enough pressure to penetrate the soft tissue. She trembled at his touch, too shocked to scream.

"It is okay," he said. "You can start screaming anytime you like."

As he pressed his dagger-like nail deeper and began to carve a line from her exposed navel to the middle of her chest, Jillian did just that.

***

Mark stood talking with a pissed-off-looking weasel in a Dodgers ball cap.

"Mark, Mark," Cindy shouted, falling into him.

"Jesus, Cindy." He held her up. "What the hell's the matter with you?"

"Excuse me, miss," the weasel said.

"Mark, it's Jill," she said

"Mr. Remme," the weasel pleaded. "We must get this start—"

"Jillian? Where is she?"

"Up in Sean's office, but the door's locked. They won't open it, and when I grabbed the doorknob..." She raised her scalded hand up to him.

"Come on." He shoved past the weasel, leaving the douchebag yelling in the background.

***

Finished, Eiddam freed her. Jillian slid from the desk to the floor. Her thoughts swirled, her vision distorted as a fog of oblivion fell over her.

The dreadful voice lanced her fading consciousness.

"*You* will open the doorway for the master," Eiddam said.

Jillian fought to keep from passing out. The flames from the candles on the desk burned higher and higher. So high they should be licking the ceiling. A ceiling she could no longer see. She craned her neck toward the door. It, too, was gone. A smoky, fluttering blackness stretched from wall to wall.

*Oh God, how am I supposed to get out?*

"This building is older than you know. It has been the gateway for many monstrosities from many realms." He brought a hand to his chest, dug his talons in, and scraped off a large patch of dissolving skin, dropping it to the floor. The tiled floor below sizzled with each plop. "This place has always attracted the vulgar, the downtrodden, those with no place else to fit in, a place for all to give into their darker cravings. You shouldn't be all that surprised. It was you and your friends that invited us."

*Invited? Us?* Jillian couldn't think straight. She felt inebriated.

"You don't even realize the power the flesh has over you."

Jillian shook her head from side to side, the feeling of violation rising again like bile.

"But you see how weak it is, yes? This—" He peeled off an area of tissue from his throat and threw it at her feet.

She scurried back, whimpering as he continued his grotesque exhibition and his vile sermon.

"This is *nothing*. This—" He pulled one of Sean's ears free "—is disposable."

She ducked as he flung it past her head, droplets of blood splashing across her left eye and the bridge of her nose.

"What do you want from me," she screamed.

"You are an innocent among the sinners. You will be the master's sacrifice." His eyes began to shine a hypnotic white light.

Jillian felt his magnetic pull. "God, please."

"Oh, my love. *He* has no place here, but you, you will be adored forever."

***

Beneath them, Cindy heard the weasel announcing Bad Obsession to the stage. The gathering throng of rockers exploded. It was the loudest crowd she'd ever heard at The Shantyman. She stood in the black hallway with Mark as they approached the office door. The knob no longer shined red, but Cindy couldn't bring herself to touch it. She found it hard to breathe up here. Like the air was a thick fog, heavy and wet.

"The door knob is ice cold," Mark said.

The thick air swirled around her. Cindy tilted, dizzy and nauseous. She stumbled off to the left.

"Cindy, are you all right?"

Mark sounded miles away rather than next to her. The room teetered. "M-Mark?"

"Cindy? Where are you? I can't see a goddamn thing."

The urge to get everyone out of the club suddenly seemed essential. "P-pull..." She coughed. Something thick and oily wrapped around her throat and slithered up to her lip. "Pull the fire ..."

"What?"

"Pull the fire alarm!" she said, the thing around her throat began closing tight.

"But there's no fire?" he said, the words slurring as they came from his mouth.

"Just do it," she managed to squeak out.

"Where the hell is it?" he asked.

"On the wall..."

"Got it!" Mark said. "You sure you want me to do this?"

"Arrrgghhh...y-y-yessss..."

***

Jillian watched in horror as the gash down her front—courtesy of the demon—began to pulse, but it did not bleed. How or why didn't matter. The entire night was beyond reason. Satisfied that her insides wouldn't spill out, she gritted her teeth and rose to her feet. Blood-spattered and shamed, she let the rage surge through her.

"Listen to them, how they worship. He will be here..." Eiddam's horns protruded from his skull, green, viscous sludge moving over the bones and muscle of what remained of Sean's body. He stretched his arms out in a Jesus Christ pose.

Jillian clutched at her faith and prayed to God that He would empower her just this once.

Guitars exploded below them. Rhythmic drums brought forth the primal and aggressive intuition within the many, the weak, the supplicant...

"Yes," Eiddam moaned. "The Master is coming..."

A deafening sound bleated out from overhead. The loud blast stunned Jillian into submission. Someone had pulled the fire alarm, but why weren't the sprinklers working?

The band below fell silent. The crowd went from screams of ecstasy to cries of panic.

It was Eiddam who now bellowed in rage.

Jillian stood, fists clenched at her side and ready to unleash her own brand of hell. She bent before the desk, clutching the cheap metal and flimsy wood in her grasp, and flipped it over. The torch-like flames shot out and set everything ablaze, invoices, magazines, the small shag rug in front of the desk. All of it caught fire.

Eiddam raised his arms over his head and wailed as the flames engulfed him.

All around them, the blackness that had started to devour the room dissipated, returning the four walls and ceiling of The Shantyman as Jillian knew them.

Eiddam fell to the floor, crawling, mewling, and reaching out toward her.

The office door flew open. Mark and Cindy stood, hands before their faces, as a viscous black cloud swirled around them before bursting into a blinding light that knocked them all to the floor.

Jillian heard Eiddam roar one final time as she was swallowed by the pain.

***

Eiddam felt his master's rage as he continued to burn.

"No...please."

*BROTHER, YOU HAVE FAILED ME FOR THE LAST TIME.*

Eiddam's bubbling flesh and charred body spilled ichor as it was stretched by the invisible beings. He groveled, but to no avail. As the overhead sprinklers finally began to discharge, Eiddam, or what remained of him, dissolved into smoke.

***

Jillian awoke in the back of an ambulance, Mark and Cindy each on one side of her, a paramedic on the other. She tried to smile but couldn't. She lay wounded, broken, confused...but alive.

**MONDAY**

Three days later, Jillian met Mark and Cindy at the club's front door. Mark had phoned her earlier to let her know the damage to The Shantyman was minimal, most of it confined to the upstairs office. She stepped from her car and took Cindy's hand.

"You look good," Cindy said.

"I'm feeling better, considering."

"It's cool that Sean and Coop left the club to you," Mark said. "When do we—"

"Never," she said. "I want nothing to do with this place."

"Woo," Mark said. "Thank God. I was hoping you'd say that. Frankly, even being this close again makes my skin crawl."

She felt it, too.

Cindy nodded along.

Jillian walked to the door. The posters for the momentous MTV Headbanger's Ball gig with Bad Obsession still plastered the entry way and the inside of the door. She pulled the keys out, gave them a once over, and then slipped them back in her purse.

"Fuck this place," she said. "Let someone else have it."

"Come on," Cindy said. "Let's go grab a drink or two or three."

"Nah, I think I'm gonna drive out to my mom's. Why don't you two go ahead."

She noticed the sparkle in Mark's eyes as the two looked at one another.

"Are you sure?" Cindy said.

"I'm sure. Go."

Cindy and Mark each gave her a hug.

"Call me, tonight, tomorrow, whenever," Cindy said. "I'm here if you need me for anything."

"Thanks. I will."

She watched them walk side by side. After a few seconds, Cindy grabbed Mark's hand. Maybe something decent came out of this after all.

Jillian climbed into her car, headed for the freeway and thought of the horrible dream she'd had last night—the demons, the black fog, a throne made of human bones, and that vulgar imitation of Sean's voice whispering in her ear.

She took the onramp and fought her way into traffic. Jillian was done with the Bay Area. She'd talked to a cousin in Riverside and had agreed to move into their recently vacated room. It was a nice complex with a fitness center, pool, and a hot tub. Hell could follow her, but it would have to catch her.

# Kelvin's World

He loved sitting in his van, reading a yellowed paperback, listening to Tom Petty on the radio and dreaming of killing his mother's nurse, Asia.

His watch told him it was nearly 7:00 p.m. His stomach growled in anger. He'd worked up a sweat putting up mother's flower boxes. He wouldn't be surprised if he had a good blister in the morning.

Kelvin Regal had to go inside. Asia's daily report awaited, along with her damned judging eyes. He killed the engine and waddled into the air-conditioned house.

"She's asleep," Asia said, her voice hard and cold, raking across his spine.

"You can go now," he said, and headed for the kitchen.

"I'll be back in the morning." She turned with her chin titled upward and strolled out the front door.

Kelvin stared out the kitchen window, wiping the cooling sweat from his forehead as she pranced across the street in her slutty, too tight skirt out to her ugly cube-shaped car.

He'd told his mother Asia was probably a hussy, and that she couldn't be but a year out of nursing school. Mother had told him she liked the girl and that she was doing fine work. Mother had also mentioned that Asia was attractive *and* single. Sure, she was decent looking. But her hair was too frizzy, and her tits were too small. At least she had an okay face and long legs. She certainly liked showing off that ass of hers too, not that he really cared. She was a judgmental bitch. That trumped all.

He couldn't help but think of their first interaction three months ago when she started.

She'd worn black yoga pants, a white Riverside High t-shirt, and her hair in a bun. Her dangly Platform 9 and 3/4 earrings were a nice touch, but when she'd caught him looking her over, she'd raised her paperwork over her chest and given him a nasty look akin to *ew, gross.* Then she'd skirted out of the room. He hadn't even said a word.

When his mother introduced them later that afternoon, she'd refused his proffered hand, barely giving him a nod or a second glance. She proceeded to ask his mother about him and why he still lived at home as if he weren't even there. He'd been so tempted to unload on her and explain that his IQ was unquestionably well above hers, but instead, he took a deep breath and excused himself. He'd headed straight for his van and drove two blocks away to the storage shed mother had rented out for the living room set after she'd taken the room for her own bedroom due to its proximity to the downstairs bathroom. He'd stayed there until he was certain the nurse bitch was gone.

Thinking of that day now brought all his irritation back.

He wiped the sweat from his eyes. The air conditioner was on the fritz again. He'd promised to get it fixed today, but right now, he was too irritated to deal with it. Maybe tonight after it cooled down some.

He made sure to check in on his mother before heading to his room. She'd been diagnosed four months ago with amyotrophic lateral sclerosis. Her muscles were in a state of atrophy, and the disease had no cure. To make things worse, she also suffered from solar urticaria, which caused her to break out in severe hives from exposure to sunlight. Therefore, the windows in her makeshift bedroom were boarded over. Kelvin imagined some of their neighbors thought them odd, the overweight, jobless, thirty-year-old son who still lived with his elderly, hobbled, and vampiric mother, a regular Bates Motel situation on the horizon, but that was their ignorance. Kelvin had taken care of the windows last summer when they'd discovered the severity of her allergy to the sun. He'd also insisted he be the one to take care of her ALS, but mother refused to burden him that way. She had a substantial amount of savings and chose to hire on a nurse. His mother was asleep on her bed. The only time she seemed completely at peace was when she slept. And her condition would only get worse. He tried not to think about that. He cranked her box fan up to high, backed out of the room and gently closed the door.

Kelvin worked up more of a sweat climbing the stairs to his room before parking his ass on his bed and picking up where he'd left off in his paperback. Somewhere between chapter twenty-two and his midnight snack, he decided to fire up his laptop and fuck with the idiots online. They were so easy. Pick a favorite writer, lay down a few cheap shots about their current book, and kick back and watch the comments roll in. He never replied to their responses. Why bother? The surprising part of it was that he had garnered a following due to his "hot takes." No one seemed to catch on that it was all bullshit. And why ruin a good thing? After dealing with all the haters he'd encountered daily throughout his entire life and enduring every fat joke ever conceived, it felt wonderful to let someone else really have it.

Tonight, he noticed something. This girl, Kim AK, was popping up on a lot of his most recent reviews. She not only agreed with his slayings of these literary giants, but tonight, she did him one better and called the author a flat-out fraud. Kelvin leaned back and clapped his hands. Grinning like Henry the Eighth, he hit reply on her latest kill shot.

*Bravo, Kim AK. Bravo. I couldn't have put it better myself.*

Kelvin shut the laptop down and went to bed still smiling.

***

The LED lights on his alarm clock read 3:24 when his mother's screech impaled him. Kelvin fought his way to his feet and clomped down the stairs. Her cries were frantic, like a horror movie that shoves you to the edge of your seat and your sanity, refusing to let go.

"Mom?" He flicked on the light as he entered her room.

She was face down on the floor. Her hands curled up beneath her as she vomited a green mucus to the carpet. No longer screaming, her eyes found his and went wide with terror. "Ay...ay...shhh..." she sputtered.

Kelvin couldn't tell if she was gagging or trying to speak, but before he could ask, everything stopped. He took two steps forward and watched the life within her go out. He didn't have to check her pulse to know that she was dead. This day had been coming, but he didn't think it would happen so soon. His first thoughts went to Mother's caretaker, Asia. Is that what she had been trying to say?

A dark thought squirmed into his head: *what if Asia did this?* It would probably be easy for her. You hear about nurses going all Angel of Death like Charles Cullen, the New Jersey nurse that killed something like forty patients.

Asia would be arriving shortly unless he called her and let her know what happened. Kelvin left the room to get something to clean mother up with before he decided exactly how he would handle this. He should call an ambulance, take the proper steps, but he wanted to confront Asia first.

He got a wetted cloth and returned to his mother's side, wiping away the nauseating fluid that had spewed from her mouth and nose. He was no doctor, but she'd probably choked on the thick mucus. As he cleansed her, he realized how little her sudden death had upset him.

He took care of her and put her back into her bed, covering her with her thick comforter.

Standing in the kitchen, sipping a diet soda, his gaze landed upon the twin pack of locks mother had insisted he purchase last summer after a rash of burglaries were reported in their neighborhood. By the time he finished his drink, a set of dark-themed ideas began to formulate in his mind.

Who was he kidding? These thoughts had been simmering since the nurse first came around.

Asia Smiley knocked on the door promptly at 5:00 a.m. Much to his dismay, Mother had made certain her nurse had a key; she let herself in after the third knock. Kelvin watched from the dark corner in the kitchen as she set her handbag down in the old wooden chair by the coatrack.

"Hello? Mrs. Regal?" She paused at the Cherrywood banister, her chin tilting upward as she looked to the second floor. He waited for her to call out to him but wasn't surprised when she couldn't bring his name to her lips.

Kelvin slipped from the shadows, watching her from the doorway as she passed the stairs, moved down the hall, and stopped at the threshold of his mother's room. She reached forward, taking the padlock he'd just installed but hadn't locked in her hand. He stepped back into the kitchen as she turned and looked around, no doubt perplexed at the new lock.

"Mrs. Regal?" she said softly.

He peered around the corner in time to see her enter mother's room. Her scream brought a smile to his face.

"Kelvin," she said. "Kelvin!"

As she came rushing down the hall, passing him in his hiding place, he watched her reach the chair and start rummaging through her bag as she continued to call out to him.

Kelvin picked up the hammer he'd used to fix the flower box yesterday, and a couple of nails from the box beside it. His palms were slick. His heart raced like a rocket. He tossed the nails to the floor at the foot of the stairs.

Startled at the sound, she gasped, staring at the nails scattered on the floor.

When she turned to see where they'd come from, Kelvin swung the hammer into the side of her head. She collapsed to the floor with a thump, her cell phone in her hand.

Kelvin set the hammer down and lifted Asia into his arms. He carried her to Mother's room and laid her on the bed.

After scrounging through the old computer room across the hall where he stored the lawn and gardening tools, his toolbox, and other random shit, he found a twine of cheap hemp rope and used it to tie Asia's hands and feet. He found a pair of pantyhose in the back of his mother's underwear drawer and tied it around Asia's mouth to keep her relatively quiet. The last thing he needed was his neighbors inquiring about screaming women in his house. *His* house.

There was an odd yet comforting feeling washing over him. For the first time in forever, he'd be free. Free of tending to the old woman and her growing needs. Free of her obvious looks of disappointment in him still living at home, no wife, no future. And soon he'd also be free of that nurse bitch. He almost felt bad for smiling.

Satisfied that Asia was secure, he closed her in the room with Mother and clicked the new padlock shut.

Taking a diet soda and a bag of Doritos up to his room, Kelvin picked up his paperback. Hell, he only had three chapters left. He'd need to toss a review up when he finished. He wasn't sure how long Asia would be out. There had been a decent amount of blood, but she'd come to eventually. But he was a creature of habit. Friday was new review day. Mother was dead, and he would have to call the hospital and let them know sooner rather than later. He'd have to get rid of Asia first. Still, he couldn't let his followers down. He could get this done in thirty minutes, then he'd take care of Asia.

While he enjoyed the majority of Scott Stripling's *Coma Girl,* he found plenty of nagging and eye-rolling moments to load into his review. Lazy writing was a pet-peeve of his, but if the characters and story were great, he let it slide. *Coma Girl* was such a story, yet he had a reputation to keep and the devil at the keyboard wouldn't have it any other way.

He managed to get the review up in twenty-one minutes. He used the spare time to wait for a response to the article. Within the ten minutes, he had several high-fiving comments, along with one angry troll calling him an asshole. It was all on par with the norm. He was disappointed there was no response from Kim AK. He'd check back in a few hours. Until then, he had company to tend to.

Pulling the lock down, he gripped the knob and eased the door open. It was dark in the boarded-up room, but it wasn't too dark to see that the nurse was gone. Kelvin stumbled into the room, bewildered and ready to lose his shit. His mother's death scent soured his senses. He pulled his t-shirt up over his nose and mouth as he hurried to the bed and clicked on the lamp. The slap of shoes across the hardwood floor caused him to turn just in time to have something that felt like a rock smash him in the forehead. He collapsed to the ground, the world turning black and filling with a pain he felt in his teeth.

Kelvin struggled to stay alert, to stay in the here and now. Crying, he tried to pick himself up from the floor. There was so much blood. He knew head wounds bled worse than other injuries, but this was beyond scary.

"Asia," he whimpered.

The lamp clicked to life.

"What were you going to do to me, Kelvin?" Asia asked.

Between the tears and the blood, his vision blurred.

"Were you going to kill me?" At his side now, she whispered into his ear, "Were you going to fuck me? I didn't have you pegged as the rapist-type—well, maybe a kiddie fiddler, but—"

"I wasn't going to do anything. I... I thought you killed her."

"You thought I killed your mom? So, you hit me with a hammer and locked me in a room, and you were just going to hold me here until I confessed, or the cops arrived?"

He was getting light-headed, the blood loss, the moment, it was all too much. "I... I don't know... I wasn't thinking clearly."

"Well, I do have a confession—you were right."

*The bitch.* He wiped the blood from his eyes and saw her reaching into her bag.

She drew out a needle and plucked off the little plastic tip, tossing it to the floor. "Would you like to join her?" she asked, walking toward him.

"No, please, I won't tell anyone."

"You are *all* bullshit, aren't you?"

"No, I won't, I swear."

She sighed. "I know you much better than you think, Kelvin."

"How would you know me? You haven't even talked to me in the six months you've been working here. You've never even been able to look me in the eyes for more than two seconds. How the fuck dare you say you know me."

She crouched next to him and flicked the end of the needle with her middle finger. "I know the kind of person you are."

"Yeah, and what kind of person am I?"

"You're a big, fat pussy."

Before he could do more than whimper, she plunged the needle into his backside.

"I don't know if you know how the internet works, but your digital footprint is pretty easy to track, KsWorld22."

"Oh, wow, you can use a computer." He knew he was in no position to fuck with her, but he was too pissed to care. "You don't know shit."

"How about the power you wield? How about the audience you command?"

"What the fuck are you talking about?" His head felt heavier. He couldn't feel his feet, and his thighs were tingling.

"You review books and albums. You tear artists apart."

"What? Are you fucking serious? Aw hell, what'd I do, point out that one of your favorite authors sucks? Come the fuck on."

"My boyfriend worked for two years on his novel. He slaved over *every* word. He stayed up night after night pouring his heart and soul into those characters and that story and you, some fucking asshole that still lives with his mother demolished him and his art in a matter of minutes."

"If he can't take criticism, he doesn't belong in the writing business. He shoulda kept his books for you and his grandmother."

"Fuck you."

"Fuck *you*," he spat. "Tell him to toughen the hell up. If he loves his own work so much, why the fuck does he care what I think?"

"You're so goddamn conceited, and it's all a fucking show," she said. A tear dropped to her lap. She got up and began digging through her purse.

Kelvin was numb from his toes to his elbows. He tried wiggling his fingers. They danced, but it was a chore to get the slightest movement from them. She was going to kill him. Unless this was some temporary paralyzing shit. Maybe she had something else in mind.

She charged forward and put a book in his face: *The Imposter* by Phillip Gehring.

*Holy hell, that piece of shit? She'd done all this because that asshole and that pile of crap couldn't take a real review?*

"You got me," he said. "I didn't like it. So what?"

She flipped the cover, revealing the author photo. He saw a beanpole of a man with greasy-looking black curls, dark-rimmed glasses, a leather jacket and the weakest chin this side of Glass Joe. "You remember Phillip? You remember this book?" She shoved it in his face.

"Yes, yes, fuck."

"You didn't just say his book sucked. You said he was one of the worst writers you'd ever read. That the prose was the work of a middle schooler armed with a thesaurus, and that he was desperate to prove he belonged. That the protagonist was among the most pathetic you'd ever read and made finishing the book a goddamn chore."

"Sounds about right. But that's just *my* opinion, and I'm entitled—"

"He's fucking dead, you asshole. He hanged himself in our bedroom closet."

"Well…" That wasn't what he expected, for sure. Still, it wasn't his fault. People don't kill themselves over one review. They have to have prior mental issues. "That is awful, but how's that my problem?"

She lashed out with her sneakered foot, the kick smashing him in the teeth. Blood filled his mouth. He felt his two front teeth with his tongue, they were now aiming inward.

"He did it because of your *powerless* words. Because of your thoughtless, entitled opinion." She began to stalk back and forth like a wild animal gearing up for an attack. "His sales stopped cold. You have an audience that listens. I know. I've been pretending to be one of them for the last couple months."

"You what?" It came out more like *ew whah?*

"Kim AK, as in Kimberly Asia Gehring is going to AK your ass into oblivion."

It was fucking crazy. *She* was fucking crazy. Her husband kills himself over a review and she goes off the fucking rails and *kills* his mother?

"Sorry he did that, but you can't put that on me," he said.

"We'll see about that." She walked out of the room, closing the door behind her.

He had to get the fuck out of here. He needed to call the police. She'd confessed to killing his mother. And she'd done it all to get to him because of a review. It was useless. He couldn't move, and now, his tongue and lips were numb. What was next? His fucking vision?

The door opened, and Asia came back into the room.

"'The tongue, as a poisonous weapon, is worse than any such weapon developed so far by human beings.' I'm not sure who said that, but it's true."

He tried to speak but couldn't make a sound. She was wearing rubber gloves and holding a pair of scissors.

"Before I was a nurse, I worked at a hair salon. These are hair cutting scissors. My best. My favorite. My sharpest. I used to cut Phillip's hair. It's how we met. He was so damn sensitive. It's what made him such an amazing person, such an amazing writer. He wore his heart on his sleeve. He was the most honest, open, empathetic, adoring man I ever met. We married the very next summer. He was already halfway through writing the manuscript for *The Imposter* when we moved to Portland. And despite what you say, he could take criticism. *Constructive* critiques were fine with him. But that's not really your style, is it, Kelvin?"

His thoughts were slow. Double vision set in. He wished it would take his hearing. He didn't want to know what she was going to hit him with next.

"You fed off the comments. Like some kind of fucking jack-off vampire, you got a hard-on over the applause from other idiots who wouldn't know a good story if it fucked them in the ass. I'm sure you had your share of mountains to climb. I'm sure you got your share of hell from what? Family? Classmates? Co-workers? Strangers? But this platform put you in the driver's seat, didn't it? *You* wielded the sword. The big stick. But you know what? You don't look before you swing.

You don't have any idea who you're hitting. You aren't striking down jocks and jerks. You're hitting others just like you. You minimized and marginalized their hurt and pain and their blood on the page, and you tore it all to shreds.

"No," she paused. "Your *review*, your *careless words* weren't the noose—Phillip had his issues—but your pointless, adore me bullshit was the boot that kicked the chair out from under him."

She eased his jaw open, then grabbed his tongue and pulled it out of his mouth. He couldn't feel a thing and could barely make out the tip of it before his blurry eyes. He could only watch in horror as she brought the scissors up and with a quick snip held his severed tongue in her hand for him to see.

"You won't have *this* to destroy people with." She brought his hand up to his eyes.

Kelvin watched, unable to close his eyelids, as she clipped his fingers off. She moved to his other hand and followed suit.

When she was finished, she dropped the scissors and pulled another phone from her pocket. His phone.

"Hi," she spoke into it. "I'm here at 211 High Street. There's a male losing blood that needs help right away. Also, an old woman has died. Please, hurry." Tossing the phone across the room, she pulled a pistol from her bag. "Your words hold power you cannot fathom. Please be careful with people. Please. You never know what that power is capable of."

His sight was blurred to epic proportions, but he heard the loud *BANG* as the gun went off, followed by the *thump* of her body hitting the floor.

Kelvin's world had been rocked.

# Comfortably Numb

Dennis Luthor entered the forest and felt his stomach curdle. Doubled over, he waited to see if the sudden sickness would settle or expel itself. Cold chills prickled the flesh on the backs of his arms. *Gooseflesh*—he'd read that word in a Hunter Shea novel. He'd never heard anyone say it in the real world, but it was quite fitting in horror fiction. It seemed apropos now, even as the sickly feeling dissipated as quickly as it had arrived.

Standing straight, he wiped the sweat from his brow and gazed into the shimmering shadows broken only by sporadic casts of golden rays that stabbed at the earth like God's fence posts. He took two steps forward when he noticed something different about these woods...*silence*. Of all the forests he'd ever played in growing up or the ones surrounding any of the campgrounds he and his dad had stayed in along the way here, this was the only time he'd ever heard perfect silence. No birds, no mosquitoes, no frogs. How could this be? The only time he could think of hearing of anything like it was in some nature documentary about forest fires. Animals could sense the danger of oncoming conflagrations and would vacate the areas at once.

Dennis sniffed the air.

No smoke. No strange smells. Just damp earth and pine trees.

Venturing further, he noticed a trail. He'd somehow missed it coming in. Maine was a land picked by God for hikers and snowmobilers. Each place he and his dad had stopped at thus far had been full of mountain bikers, couples, and families getting in their "steps" and enjoying the great outdoors. *Vacationland*, that's what the sign read as they'd crossed into the state. He agreed. The place really held a natural excitement. It didn't need skyscrapers or movie stars to make itself attractive.

Dennis quickly forgot the peculiar vibes of this particular patch of woods and became enamored by its beauty. He was surrounded by maples, hemlocks, and pines along with the most ferns he'd seen growing in one area. It almost felt like he was on the forest moon of Endor. He half-expected to see an Ewok any minute now. The shade from the taller trees along the path kept the August heat at bay, and the quiet left Dennis alone with his thoughts.

Dad sold the mobile home at the start of summer. They left the Azalea Trailer Park Plaza (which sounded much more luxurious than it was) in Savannah, Georgia, on June 1st and headed north in the tiny RV his dad bought off a buddy from his last job. The thing smelled like mildew and old hot dogs, but like most of the things Dennis had to deal with, he acclimated quickly and rolled with it. They made frequent stops, sometimes only going two or three towns over to the next RV campsite as his dad left him kicking around whatever little town or village they visited while he went scouring for job opportunities.

Last month, they'd stayed in a place in Virginia for almost two weeks before getting run off the campground after his dad knocked out some loud redneck over a woman. "Defending her honor" was what his dad called it. Dennis knew better. More likely his father fucked around with the guy's wife and got caught. Dad hadn't been much of a gentleman since mom left him. He took care of Dennis all right, but everything else in his father's life was spur of the moment one minute, gone to hell the next.

His dad didn't like being told what to do. Working under holier than thou (Dad's words) bosses with small pricks and Little Big Man syndrome (also his father's words) was not his dad's cup of tea but seemed to be the only work he could ever land. It was never too long before his dad's rage set in and they were moving on.

Savannah had been different—for a few months. Working at Georgia Transformer under a supervisor he got along with (Reggie, the former owner of the mildew and old hot dog smelling RV), dad paid for six months up front at the trailer park and looked to be settling in. Dennis had quit school before the start of his junior year, so he needed to find work within walking distance. Dad never made him get jobs, but Dennis had wanted to support his reading habit, so he'd needed to suffer through hours of shitty things like flipping burgers and washing dishes.

A tent just off the path broke him from his reverie, delivering a fresh splash of goosebumps along his spine. The ferns had thinned out here, leaving a more barren appearance. Here, the shadows easily outnumbered the sunlight. The tent's bright yellow nylon fabric stood out among the backdrop of fallen trees and dark soil. There seemed an odd number of felled trees. As if a storm had blown through not too long ago and knocked this area silly.

Dennis gazed back toward where he'd come from and saw a fog had settled over the path. He'd not noticed that, either. Only the absolute quiet remained the same.

Looking over at the tent, he wondered if someone was inside. The thought of calling out and hearing his own voice seemed sacrilegious out here, as if disturbing the silence would welcome the wrath of the woods. He imagined hundreds of sets of red eyes coming to life in the shade of the trees. Or worse, coming to life in the mist.

After a few seconds of fighting his better instincts, he said, "Hello?"

The tiniest static, almost like the sound of a thousand people breathing in unison through clenched teeth, built off in the distance: a radio signal just coming into range. The fog closed in behind him.

Stepping off the path, he called out again.

A light breeze swept past him. He saw a corner of the rain protector atop the tent wave a couple of times before falling flat again.

"Is there anybody in there?" he asked.

This time he heard his question repeated back to him behind the increasingly audible static, *"Is there anybody in there?"*

An echo? Or someone or something mimicking him? Dennis couldn't tell, and he didn't dare to find out. He dreaded it being the latter. He'd read enough supernatural stories where grown men pissed themselves, and he most certainly did not want to join that particular club. If anyone was in the tent, they were either asleep, not there, or ignoring him. Whatever the case, he decided to push on.

The fog caught up with him as the trail veered right.

The static sound disappeared. Had he imagined it? This whole thing was starting to trip him out like some kind of freaky dream. He was about to turn back and head to the RV when he saw something dangling from one of the trees ahead.

The fog rolled up around his legs like a ghost wrapping him in the strange mist. He gazed beyond the ground cloud at the thing hanging from the tree.

Feet.

*Fuck this.*

The fog swallowed the sight before he could be certain.

*"Is there anybody in there?"* the echo from earlier—his voice, or some mimic of it—called out from beyond.

And then again, *"Is there anybody in there?"* This time it was a short, dragging noise. Back and forth. Back and forth. It sounded less like his own and instead resembled a song he'd heard on his dad's record player, something about being numb. It was a haunting track, but right now, that was the last thing he wanted to hear.

The dragging sound came again. Back and forth. *Back and forth.*

"Hello?" he asked.

Something moved through the fog.

*No fucking way.*

He turned and started back the way he came, but he couldn't find the trail.

*"Hello, hello, hello..."*

"Who's there?" he shouted, his voice cracking as he found a tree and held on to it just to hold something solid, something tangible, something here.

The only sound was the back and forth dragging.

Whatever was hanging from that tree, it was making that sound. He recognized it now. His grandpa used to have a tire swing in the front yard. That was the same noise it made when Dennis used to swing on it. He remembered one of the last times he'd been there thinking the rope would break while he was on it.

What if he *had* seen feet? Could that really have been a person hanging from the tree? He thought of the tent, whether it could be the murderer or the victim. The need to know rose in him like bile, unwanted yet unstoppable.

*Prove it,* he thought to himself. *Prove that it's a body. Prove you're not being fucking crazy and panicking because you're lost in the woods.*

He let go of the tree and started toward the noise.

*Back and forth.*

He saw a shape slowly swaying up ahead. He gasped as it stopped.

The silence returned like an invisible weight pressing against his sanity.

He could see the dark leggings, and a bare foot. The other foot had a hiking boot strapped to it.

Moving closer, his insides demanded that he turn back. Dennis reached for the body, the mist still swirling around him like a breathing thing.

*"Is there anybody in there?"*

The voice from the record came again. He was getting turned around. He tried peering into the fog.

Something thudded to the ground behind him.

Holding his breath, he looked over his shoulder, ready to see the dead woman standing there...but the body was gone. Above him, the rope began to swing, *back and forth*.

He glanced at the ground and saw the other hiking boot.

Not giving a fuck if he was on the trail or not, Dennis ran. He just wanted to get as far away as he could.

Branches clawed at his face, stinging his flesh as he plowed through the thicket. The path was there, then it wasn't.

*I turned right somewhere up here.*

Once he found the path again, he slowed. The bend was just ahead. From there it was a straight shot... Wait, no, that wasn't correct. He'd found the trail after coming through from the edge of the parking lot to the little grocery store.

His heart hammered inside his chest.

*This goddam fog...*

If it didn't clear up or go away to wherever the hell it came from, he would be wandering around out here until nightfall. His mind conjured up bears and mountain lion, and killers with knives ready to hack him up and hang him.

He slowed to catch his breath and heard something approaching from behind.

*Step. Drag. Step. Drag.*

Glancing over his shoulder. A figure began to emerge from the ground cloud.

Dennis bolted.

This time he ran with complete reckless abandon. The trail vanished, and he was tripping over roots and stumbling blind, desperate to escape.

*"Hello, hello, hello..."*

Laughter.

*Step. Drag. Step. Drag*

Breathing as heavily as he was and making as much noise stomping through the brush, he shouldn't be able to hear the thing walking after him. But it came through loud and clear.

*Back and forth. Back and forth.*

Dennis screamed for all he was worth.

He ran into something in his way and tumbled forward. Tangled up, he fell and rolled to a stop. His head slammed hard against the ground.

***

When he opened his eyes, the fog was gone.

He saw what had tripped him up. The tent laid upside down next to him. Its little fabric door hung open so he could see what was inside, a single sheet of white paper.

He reached in and gently, as if damaging it could bring the entire world to an end, he picked it up and brought it out into the daylight.

*Dear Mom and Dad,*

*This isn't the world you brought me into. This isn't the world I thought would be so amazing when I grew up. Not only do I not like this world, I don't belong...*

Dennis didn't read the rest; he skipped to the end.

It was signed–*Jane*

It had been her back there along the path. A deep sorrow flooded his body, his mind, his soul.

Looking down at the note, a tear plopped next to her name.

Dennis set the piece of paper down, flipped the tent right side up and located the three pegs he'd knocked loose. He sunk them back into the earth where they'd been before he knocked them free. Picking up the note, he placed it inside as Jane had left it.

His knees scuffed, a lump bulging from the top of his forehead, Dennis found the trail and stared ahead. In his mind he heard her final refrain: *Back and forth. Back and forth.*

***

Dennis walked from the trees into the busy parking lot feeling like he'd been gone for days rather than the ninety or so minutes. Two local punks were sharing a forty and laughing at him as he locked eyes with the one with a shaved head.

"Dude," the kid said. "Are you fucking nuts?"

Dennis stared at him.

"What'd you see, man?" the other kid with dyed blue bangs asked.

"What?" Dennis asked, unsure whether he should give a rat's ass what they were going on about. "What do you mean?"

The shaven-headed guy pointed behind him.

Dennis turned and saw it, a sign that read "Keep out!" Below that someone had painted: "Ease Your Pain Gardens. Home to the estranged and the forgotten."

# OUT OF RANGE

**I.**

The day they killed the Internet, we knew our time was short. The signal piped in from somewhere out there. They announced their existence.

The lone broadcast came in on March 27, 2016. It was the last thing our satellites would send or receive. On every device across the world, we saw them, three human looking beings. Black hair, slightly longer faces, slim arms, narrow waists, and beady eyes that challenged Clint Eastwood's "Go ahead, Punk" glare. The message was short, but crystal clear: "Your world is not yours. We gave it life as we gave you. We are coming home."

No one that saw the initial broadcast, which played on a five-minute loop, felt it was real until none of us could share it or tweet it or watch it again. We thought the Russian hackers had gotten bored with their constant breaches into our credit card accounts and grown tired of their successful cyber break-ins into important government agencies. Now they had somehow made a Hollywood-style production to fuck with us in a new entertaining way.

We were wrong.

That was two months ago. They haven't come yet, and it's a damn good thing. We sure as fuck aren't ready.

"What did they say again?" my nephew asked. He was excited in all the ways the rest of humanity was not.

"They are coming," I said.

"Uncle Nick, what else?"

"The rest was—"

"Wendi told me they said they made Earth"

"Come on, Jack, get some sleep."

"Wendi said they made us."

"Your sister says a lot, doesn't she?"

"Uncle Nick?"

"Yeah, bud?"

"If they made *us*, what did *God* do?"

"God made the universe, Jack. Get some sleep."

I leaned forward, kissed his forehead, and moved to the door.

"Uncle Nick?"

"Yeah, bud?"

"I hope they're nicer than Wendi says."

"Me too, buddy. Me too."

I shut the light and closed his door.

My sister Lindsay sat comatose, curled up in the recliner in the living room. I had moved in with her and the kids a few weeks ago. Jack and Wendi needed me, and I just wanted to make sure Lindsay didn't burn the fucking place down in her haze.

"Wendi call yet?" My question hung like ready spaghetti to the wall and fell just as fast. Lindsay was someplace else. Wendi was a great kid for a sixteen-year-old. I knew I didn't have to worry about her, but that never stopped me.

I went to the kitchen, grabbed a Pabst from the fridge and snagged the old school rotary phone from the end table. I glanced at the TV. Lindsay had her *Grey's Anatomy* DVD collection on an endless loop, though I'm not sure how much of the show she was actually absorbing. Lindsay's brain seemed to have crashed shortly after the demise of the World Wide Web.

I swung the cord of the phone under the cheap trailer door and placed the ugly pea green antique next to me. Unattractive, but they should be used for practicality only! Cell phones were now flashlights, mp3 players, and cameras, nothing more.

I guzzled the tall boy and stared up at the constellations that dressed the night sky. As I had every night since they contacted us, I wondered where they were. Were they fucking with us already? Or were they really that far away? Was this all a part of their plan to make us wonder these questions? Make us paranoid? Drive us to the edge and see how long we could last before we went *Full Metal Jacket* and blew our brains out?

I grabbed the pack of cigarettes from my front shirt pocket and twirled it between my thumb and forefinger. I'd quit last year. There were worse relapses to be had, though. I slipped the Bic from my jeans and lit the smoke.

The phone blared to life, and I jumped.

"Hello?"

"Hey, Uncle Nick."

"Hey, Wendi."

"Just calling to let you know I'm on my way home."

"Thanks. You have a good time?"

"Something strange happened."

"Huh? Like what? What do you mean?"

"I...I'll tell you when I get home."

"You need a ride?"

"No. I'm fine. Will you be there when I get home?"

"Yeah. Unless Eye Patch comes back to finish me off."

"Who?"

"No one. You be safe. I'll be here."

"Okay, bye."

I wondered what, in lieu of our current situation, might qualify as strange.

***

Wendi came up the driveway forty-five minutes later with another blast from the past piece of technology in her hands. Her long, brown hair spread over her Alkaline Trio sweatshirt. She walked up to the steps with a large, gray boom box in her hands. She set it on the bottom step and took up some porch next to me.

"Did you lug that thing all the way from your friend's house?" I asked.

"Yep."

It was just like one I had when I was twelve. Big gray box. AM/FM Radio, cassette deck, built-in mic.

"Bet you had one just like it."

"Uh-huh."

"You've been out here this whole time, haven't you?"

"Uh-huh." I pulled another Pabst from the ring.

She raised her gaze to the starry night above. "I think they're here."

A chill slithered down my spine. "What?"

"I don't think they want us to know yet."

"What makes you say that?"

"I don't know. It just feels right."

Wendi had a knack for calling things, a gift for intuition. Her gut had a freaky way of acting like Nostradamus on steroids. She'd known her dad had been in an accident before the call even came through. She'd known he'd been out buying her the field hockey stick she'd begged him for before the tractor trailer demolished his new Ford Focus. She also knew whenever it was going to pour, even when the sun was shining. Premonitions, Spidey-Sense, however you put it, she had it. This time, I hoped she was off.

I took another swig. "You said something strange happened. I'm assuming you mean besides you coming home with this boom box."

"Yes."

"Care to elaborate?"

She turned her blue eyes to me. "Do you think God's real?"

"I don't know. I hope so."

Her eyes gleamed in the twilight. Her lower lip trembled.

"Come 'ere."

She slid over and leaned her head on my shoulder. I didn't press her.

"I want Him to be. I want..." Her voice quivered.

I set down my beer and squeezed her hand.

"I want to see my dad again." Her body shook.

I felt the tears roll down my cheeks. We sat that way for a time.

"Thank you," she said.

"For what?"

"For being here."

"Whenever you need me," I said.

"Do you have a cigarette?"

"What?"

She sat up and wiped her eyes with the sleeve of her sweatshirt. "You heard me."

I tapped one from my pack and handed it to her. "When did you start doing this?"

"I don't know. Last month?"

I lit it for her and grabbed my beer. "So, you were saying."

She exhaled. "No, I wasn't."

"I see how it is."

"Okay." She took another drag and looked at me. "I think I heard something."

"What do you mean? What, what did you hear?"

"Carrlyn and I were fooling with that." She nodded to the radio. "It was in their basement, and we were just messing around with the button when we heard it."

"Heard what?"

"This...voice."

"What? A radio signal?"

"No. I mean, I don't know. It sounded like..."

"Like?"

"Like a walkie-talkie, like me and Jack used to use. This voice broke in and said, *watching them...*"

"Watching them?"

"Yeah, but it..." Her blue eyes glistened.

"Wendi, what is it?"

"The voice. It was kind of fuzzy, you know, like it was barely coming in, but it sounded just like my dad." She wiped her eyes again and sucked down what remained of the cigarette.

"Maybe...maybe it was. I mean, maybe it was like one of those EVPs. Remember that movie we watched last summer, *White Noise*?"

"I don't think so."

"You don't believe—"

"I think it was one of *them*."

"Did it say anything else?"

"No, Carrlyn freaked and shut it off. I turned it back on, but whatever it was it had disappeared."

She leaned forward, hefted the boom box by its handle, and climbed the steps.

"Wait a sec." I sat my beer down and went to my car. I opened the trunk and pulled up a white cardboard box. There were two cassette tapes resting on top of some old comics. I walked back to where she stood holding the clunky radio. The sight was almost comical. "Here." I handed her the tapes.

She spread them like a hand of blackjack. "Concrete Blonde? And Kiss?"

"Yeah, you might like Concrete Blonde. Chick singer. Great voice."

She slid the tapes into her pocket. "Thanks, Uncle Nick. Think I'm gonna head to bed."

"Goodnight, Wendi."

She turned for the door and then stopped. "Is my mom up?"

"Yeah. Sort of."

"She's trying to escape, isn't she? Like if she takes enough pills, she can outrun whatever's coming. Like she can drive out of range."

"Makes sense."

"I wish she wouldn't. Goodnight, Uncle Nick."

Sixteen going on thirty. I started to smile until I remembered what she'd said: *I think it was one of them.*


## II.


"Uncle Nick, Uncle Nick!"

"Huh? What is... What is it?"

"It's back."

I rubbed the boogers out of my eyes. Wendi hovered over the couch. I sat up and saw that Lindsay had found her way to bed.

"Come on, quick."

I followed her down the hall toward the golden glow coming from her room at the end. "What time is it?"

"It's like 4 a.m."

"Have you been to sleep?"

"Yes, maybe. I don't remember."

Her bedroom was clean. Only her bed looked tussled. Some of her stuffed animals remained on top of the deep purple comforter.

Rudolph and Hermie were on the floor trying to escape beneath the bed skirt. The boom box sat dead center of the mattress.

"I was listening to the tape you gave me when I dozed off. I don't know for how long, but then this thing started making a crackling noise."

"Anything else?"

"That got my eyes open. So I looked and the play button was still down. The machine was just hissing. Then I heard him again. I heard *them* again."

"What did it say?"

"All I heard was *'something at hand.'*"

"Something at hand?"

"No, I added the something. The radio crackled, and I couldn't understand what the voice said. All I made out was *'at hand.'*"

"What are you guys doing?"

I turned and saw Jack standing in the doorway, rubbing his half-closed eyes, dressed in his Ninja Turtle PJs.

"Go back to bed, Jackie," Wendi said.

"She's right, bud. Come on, it's not morning yet."

He turned and let me usher him back into the hall.

*"We are ready."*

The hair stood on the back of my neck. My stomach dropped.

"Wendi?" Jack slipped past me and ran to the bedside. "Was that...?"

"No," she said.

"But that sounded just like..."

Her brow furrowed. She took Jack's hands in her own.

"BAAAAHHHHHHHH!" The sound exploded from the speakers like an air raid siren.

Jack flew into his sister's arms. Wendi clutched him.

I ran over and flipped the radio switch to off and killed the signal.

"What was that?" Jack said.

I went to the window. It was still dark out. I started back to the bed when it hit me. I returned to the window—I was right. No stars. The sky, littered with them only a few hours ago, was now empty.

"What is it?" Wendi said.

I let the blind fall. "It's—"

There was a boom. A whooshing, resonating boom. The trailer began to vibrate beneath my feet.

"Uncle Nick?" Jack said.

Light burst beyond the blind at my back. Brilliant white light spilled in from around the loose sides of the shade.

Jack began to whine.

"Mom?" Wendi said.

The trailer began to rattle and hum.

I heard the front door open. "Stay he—"

Jack ran for the hall.

I reached out but came up with his dust.

"Stay here," I said to Wendi. "I'll go get him."

I stepped into the hallway. The light that filled the living room was like staring out at a field of pure white snow reflecting in the sun at midday. I shielded my eyes with my hand and hurried after Jack.

Wendi followed after me.

I stopped at the end of the hall, hit by the impossibility at the door.

"Daddy!" Jack said.

"I've come for you. Each of you," a thing that looked like my sister's dead husband said.

"Jackie, Mom, no," Wendi said.

I blocked her path.

Lindsay's hands trembling over her lips as she walked into its arms. Jack ran to it as well before I could kick the shock. Before our eyes, the impossible reunion commenced.

"Jackie?" Wendi said.

The thing holding them turned its head toward us. Its beady eyes smiled to match the slight upturn of its thick lips.

The light flashed. And then they were gone.

"No!" Wendi screamed.

"Back, back, back, go," I said. I pushed her toward the back door. "Go, go, go."

I continued to guide her toward the back exit. That booming whoosh came in like a wave. The trailer shuddered.

Wendi opened the door. I stepped past her. The backyard was clear.

"Come on." I took her hand and pulled her along.

I dared a look at the sky. Rows and rows of perfectly aligned stars stretched out above us. They weren't stars.

"What is it?"

I ignored Wendi and hurried us around the corner of the trailer. Another flash of light exploded from the closest neighbor's place on the left.

"Come on."

I could see Wendi's profile tipped upward. I got us to my car, opened the passenger door, and guided her in.

I slammed the door, ran to the other side, and climbed in.

"Where are they? Where did they go? Where are they?"

*She's going into shock. I have to get us out of here.*

I started the car, threw it in gear, and spun it around on the front lawn.

"Where are they?" she said again.

I stamped the gas to the floor. The car shot down the road. My eyes darted left and right. Each home we passed seemed to light up and be hit with a bright flash like the one that took Lindsay and Jack.

"They're taking them," I spoke aloud, unsure whether Wendi would hear it or not. I just needed to say it.

More houses and trailers zipped by. More flashes.

I leaned forward and gazed up. The lights were still there.

"We shouldn't be here," Wendi said.

"Hey, stick with me."

"Is it the rapture?"

I thought about the rapture, or at least what I knew of it. The beginning of the end. Old school Bible. Scary as hell. End of days. Judgement day. My mind logged the Schwarzenegger references.

"Are they going to Heaven?"

"No," I said.

"Are *we*?"

A car swerved from the road on the right in front of us. "Hold on to something," I said.

*Hope.*

"They've come to take *us* home?" she asked.

"Not exactly."

Another car blasted out in front of us from between the old Jefferson home, and the fence surrounding Ted Berry's horses.

"Hold on!" I cranked the wheel and stamped the brake.

Tires squealed. The back end swung around. We crashed side to side into the other car. Both vehicles were forced in a diagonal direction and off the road.

I saw our feelings reflected on the couple in the other vehicle. Shock, awe, confusion.

The car stalled as it bumped and jostled to a stop in the large yard of the house across the street.

The other car raced forward and smashed head-on into a pine tree at the property's edge. Something launched through the windshield and vanished into the woods.

"What do we do?"

I looked into my niece's blue eyes. I opened my mouth, but I found no words fit.

The booming whoosh rolled over us again.

I grabbed her palsied hands. "I love you," I said.

"I love you, too."

"Close your eyes."

She did. I stared at her face a second longer and then followed my own instruction.

The car, or maybe it was the Earth, began to vibrate. White light blossomed beyond my eyelids. In my mind, I saw Jack's face.

Heaven never seemed so far away.

# MOLLY

## NIGHT ONE

His job at the Hilton was bullshit. Some of his co-workers were assholes, and the guests were even worse. Two months ago, Caleb left his cozy little night audit job at the Super 8. Sure, his nights at the sleazy property on Elmore Avenue were full of Earth scum galore—hookers, junkies, real shitty humans—but at least they kept to themselves. They stayed out of your business, and you stayed out of theirs. The same could not be said of the businessmen and women that frequented the fancy hotel in Oakman. It was a land of uppity fucks.

"Excuse me."

Lifting his gaze from the comic in his hands, he knew the voice, knew the goddamn "diamond member" tone.

*Anne Marie.*

"Oh," she said, "you *do* realize you're working, right?" She was holding a little black bucket. "Do you have a bigger ice bucket than this puny thing?"

They did, but at this moment, Caleb wasn't about to fork it over. "Nah, sorry. That's all they give us."

"So..." She looked over her shoulder.

*Shit*. He'd left the door to the hotel's meeting space open. A large red Igloo cooler was sitting atop the first table.

"Oh, yeah. I always forget about that one."

"Mmm hmm. I'm sure," she said.

"I'll just make sure it's clean. Where would you like me to bring it?"

She turned and walked toward the elevators. Without looking back, she said, "I want it filled and set out for us on the lobby table." The elevator doors opened. She stepped in, did an about face, and smiled. "We'll be down in fifteen minutes."

No please. No thank you. The door closed.

What he wanted to do was fill the fucking thing with piss.

His front desk manager, Justin, came out from the back office. "Was that Anne Marie?"

"Yeah, she wants me to clean and fill the cooler for them."

"She's one of our favs around here, Caleb. Be sure to do as she says."

Gritting his teeth, Caleb imagined beating the snot out of the prick.

Justin pushed his glasses up his nose. "I know this is a big change for you, coming from that *motel*, but our clientele is a bit more...sophisticated. They pay good money to stay here. I hope you can appreciate that."

"Yeah, I guess," Caleb muttered.

*Prick.*

"What's that?" Justin said.

"I'll get it ready for them."

"Be sure you do," Justin said. He vanished behind the wall.

Caleb cleaned the cooler, filled it with ice and the twelve-pack of Bud Light that Justin purchased for the group on the hotel's behalf, and left it on the large table by the lobby TV. Sure enough, they sauntered down at promptly 6:15. Anne Marie, the queen bitch, and her getaway lover, Isaac—an over-muscled, P-90 X douchebag—sat down first. They were definitely fucking. Caleb had seen them making out in front of Anne Marie's room before she pulled him inside by the crotch of his pants. Lizzy and Donna rounded out the little tribe. Lizzy was a bubbly blonde that seemed like the type to go along with anything. Donna was a bit older than the others, twice as hot, but mean as fuck. Long black hair, perfect curves, and legs she loved to show off in tight little business skirts, a real-life Black Widow. It wasn't long before Justin came out of the back office and joined them, whispering, and staring daggers in Caleb's direction. Their cackles echoed, carrying like rabid bats threatening him with their infection.

An hour later, Justin grabbed his keys, said his goodbyes to Anne Marie's crew before turning to Caleb. "Make sure you clean the lobby before shift change. I don't want Stephen to have to deal with this shit. He'll throw a hissy fit."

"Oh, we love Stephen," Lizzy said.

*Of course they do.*

Stephen was another fucking winner. A grade-A douchebag convinced that he did everything at the hotel, frequently branding the rest of his co-workers as lazy and incompetent.

Justin whispered something into Anne Marie's ear. She craned her head in Caleb's direction and laughed.

Justin hugged her and headed out the door.

*Good fucking riddance.*

They continued for the next forty minutes being loud and obnoxious as always, blasting bad dance songs from their phones and laughing and swearing up a storm until they finally went back up to their rooms. The lobby table was a disaster of Chinese food containers and beer cans. Caleb left it there.

He kept his head down, plowed through his second shift checklist, and was making the cash drop just as Stephen came through the lobby doors. Caleb grabbed his sweatshirt from the coat rack, punched out, and passed the desk.

"What's with the mess in the lobby?" Stephen asked.

"Justin said to have you clean it up," Caleb said.

"Oh, wonderful."

Heading out the door, walking across the wet pavement, a cool wind blew his shaggy bangs across his forehead. On impulse, he looked over his shoulder at the four-story building. A silhouette in the top corner room stood before the lit window. A person holding a small child. The light died out as the curtain fell. The sight sent a tendril of fear crawling up Caleb's spine. That was Anne Marie's room.

*Why did I think she was holding a kid?*

A car horn blared and brought him back to reality

He was standing in the middle of the parking lot, looking like a pervert staring up at the hotel windows.

"Get outta the way, moron," a man with a New York accent barked from behind the wheel of a shiny Dodge Challenger

"Sorry."

The car and its New York loudmouth jerked around him.

"Fucking kids," the man said.

Caleb got in his Kia, pulled up Van Halen's "Hot for Teacher" on his iPhone, hit play, and backed out. The light in Anne Marie's room was on again. He stamped the brakes and stared. His jaw dropped.

Behind the sheer curtain, a set of curves stood, a second silhouette. A man appeared before her, dropping to his knees.

*Isaac.*

Caleb watched as the hands roamed over her body. Caleb's dick stiffened. Now, he really was that pervert.

He pulled his gaze away, let off the brake, daring one last peek at the window. They'd moved away, but something else caught his eye. The small child was there.

The light died.

Dressed in goose bumps, he headed home.

***

Anne Marie watched Isaac slip from the sheets, pull on his underwear, slacks, and t-shirt. He was fun and beautiful. And he could fuck like a beast. It would be a shame to have to do what needed to be done. As hot as he was, the man had more brains in his cock than in his head. Their little fuck-affair was a secret. Lizzy was clueless about, well, everything, but Donna, Justin, and that dickwad, Caleb, knew better. She'd seen Caleb just this past week catch her with her boy-toy in the doorway.

That was all right, she had plans for him, too.

Her job up here in dead as fuck Maine would be finished tomorrow, and then she and Molly were off to the Caribbean.

Isaac tiptoed to the door. Lights bled into the darkened room, cracking over Molly's face.

Molly.

The darkness returned as Isaac shut the door.

Anne Marie sat up. Molly's silhouette moved.

"Come here, baby," Anne Marie said.

The doll crossed the room, a shadow in the night, and climbed up into bed. Anne Marie held the sheets up, allowing the doll to take Isaac's spot.

Molly laid still, the stitched red smile in perfect place upon her pale face.

Anne Marie covered her with the sheet, kissed her forehead, and snuggled up next to her. "You'll show them, won't you, Molly?"

She traced the doll's blood-red smile with her finger, and then closed her eyes.

***

Donna, clad in a red leather thong and nothing else, pulled Lizzy's night shirt over the trembling blonde's head. She dropped the cotton shirt to the floor, placed her hands on the woman's tan shoulders, and eased her back on the bed.

"Shh," Donna said. "No one is going to find out, okay? This is our little secret."

Lizzy, biting her bottom lip, nodded.

Donna slipped out of the thong and kicked it aside. "You're going to go first."

She loved the nervous energy radiating from the Lizzy. A few drinks and a little Benadryl and the woman was putty in her hands. Well, almost. Under the concoction's spell, Lizzy'd confessed that while she'd never been with woman, she had fantasized about it. Donna decided that was all the *yes* she needed.

She straddled Lizzy's hips. Taking her time, she let her fingers trace the young woman's nubile body.

"You have beautiful tits," Donna said.

Lizzy gave a weak smile. "Thanks."

Donna bent down, tracing the erect nipples with her lips, first one then the other. Lizzy took in a sharp breath. Donna smiled and went to work, knowing the perfect nibble to tongue-flick ratio to get the woman's motor running. She continued, slipping one hand between Lizzy's legs. Intoxicated by Lizzy's heavy breathing, quiet moans and the way she squirmed at her touch, Donna pulled her fingers from Lizzy pussy and sucked the juices from them, before bending and kissing Lizzy full on the mouth. Their tongues darted and writhed against each other. Donna broke the kiss and sat up, sliding her slick, shaved pussy up Lizzy's warm flesh.

"Your turn," she said.

Lizzy smiled and nodded.

Donna got up and wrapped her knees on either side of Lizzy's head.

Now it was Donna's turn to purr, moan, and cum.

# NIGHT TWO

Caleb's night had been a doozy. He'd arrived to work late this afternoon after getting his third speeding ticket of the year. He caught a rash of shit from Justin, and then he had to watch Angie, one of his cooler co-workers, bust out in tears after finding out something horrible about her fiancé. She never said what it was before becoming a complete mess and being sent home by Justin. Now Caleb was on his own and every nutjob in the area seemed to be trying to either get a room (two clowns, high as fuck, and demanding he match the price of the Motel 6 across the street) or was stirring up shit in the parking lot (a group of local rednecks in pickup trucks decided to get in a shouting match with two black guests). Oakman wasn't known for its crime, but there seemed to be something in the air tonight.

Before he could look up whether he was in jeopardy of losing his license, Caleb's favorite guests stumbled in through the lobby doors.

Anne Marie's tits were just about falling out of her low-cut blouse. Caleb spied her left areola and felt his face flush.

"Oh," Anne Marie said. "See something you like?"

Isaac whispered something in her ear before helping her to stand up straight.

Caleb saw Donna through the lobby door having a cigarette out by the smoker's bench.

"You know," Anne Marie said. "You could be cute...if you weren't such a fucking little prick."

"Whoa, shhh shhh," Isaac said. "Come on, let's get you upstairs."

"I'm fine, I'm fine," she said. She shoved Isaac back toward the stairwell. "You're drunker than I am. Why don't you go to bed?"

Isaac looked at her, waiting.

"Go on."

"Seriously?" he said.

"That's right, Isaac. Go sleep it off."

When she turned back to the desk, her face had gone stern. Her green eyes were mesmerizing. Caleb tried to swallow, but his mouth was dry. His nerves were all over the place.

The corners of Anne Marie's red lips turned upward.

He was frozen. He could feel his pulse throbbing in his neck.

The lobby doors rattled open.

Donna held up a six-pack of Bud Light. "Hey, stop eye-fucking that boy and come drink these with me."

Anne Marie gave him a wink and turned. "Yeah, yeah. I'm coming."

Caleb tried his best to focus on his computer, blindly scrolling through his Facebook feed, but he couldn't keep his eyes off Anne Marie. It was like his brain and his body were betraying him. He'd hated this bitch since the first day her company placed the work group at the hotel. He'd overheard Isaac and Donna mentioning that this was their last week at this job. Caleb surmised the group was heading elsewhere and couldn't wait. But was it possible he'd wanted Anne Marie the whole time? The thought repulsed and excited him.

And tonight, *"you could be cute..."* That wink and the smile. *"See something you like?"*

By 9:30, now joined by Lizzy, the three women headed for the elevator. Only Lizzy said good night. He collected their cans from the table and wiped down the area.

***

Anne Marie said good night to Donna and Lizzy and headed for Isaac's room. He'd wanted to fuck her one last time, especially with them parting ways in the morning, but she had other plans. She knocked on his door.

He was smiling as he let her in.

"Sit down," she said.

He tried to snake his arms around her, but she slapped him hard across the face and repeated the command.

Isaac, holding his meaty hand to his reddened cheek, looked ready to cry.

*Pussy.*

"I get it, all right? I have a family, but we should—"

"Shut your fucking mouth."

He fell silent, his shoulders slumped.

She set her red handbag next to him. "We've had some fun, haven't we? Don't answer that." She took a seat on the bench against the wall. "All this time and you never once told me you loved me."

"I..."

He tried to say it, but she knew he couldn't. Which didn't mean shit to her; she'd never felt a thing for him, either.

"That's okay, Isaac. I know you're incapable of loving anyone besides yourself. Your poor wife. Does she know what a slut you are?"

He went to open his mouth.

"Don't," she said.

She stood and walked toward the bathroom. "Isaac, there's someone I'd like for you to meet."

"What?"

Anne Marie flicked off the room's main light.

Molly's silhouette stood before the room's window. Something gleamed in her hand.

Anne Marie smiled and went to Isaac. She pulled his chin up and kissed him.

His hands found her ass.

She lowered her lips to his ear. "Okay, big boy. Put your hands over your head."

"I knew it, hell yes, I knew it," he said.

Anne Marie produced a set of handcuffs from her bag at the end of the bed. She cuffed his wrists and trailed a finger down his chest.

"That's so fucking hot," he said.

She felt his big prick press against her thigh.

"I can't believe we waited so long to role play."

She grabbed a second set of cuffs and a piece of rope from the bag.

"Oh, baby," he said. "Don't you even worry. I took a shit ton of Viagra. You're gonna cum and cum again."

Anne Marie held the handcuffs in her teeth as she undid his khaki's and pulled the waistband of his underwear down, releasing "Kong." She teased him, letting her lips drag across his jizz-drooling cock.

He moaned and pressed himself against her.

On the floor, she cuffed his ankles and tied the rope through the chain. She tossed the rope under the bed and felt it pull taut.

Anne Marie crawled back up and took him in her mouth.

"Hey, who...oh, god," he moaned. "You are so fucking good. You, oh ... Ah...hey, wait? What the fuck? Who is that?"

Her lips made a loud smacking sound as she came up for air. She reached into her bag of tricks and brought out the roll of duct tape. She stretched out a piece, tore it off, and slammed it over Isaac's mouth as he struggled, the cuffs on his wrists now tightly bound beneath the bed to the ones at his ankles.

She lit the candle he kept on his nightstand,

Molly sat beside him. He was stretched across the bed, bound and at their mercy. His eyes looked ready to explode from their sockets. He began squirming and flopping, a dying fish frying on the hot concrete, knowing something was exponentially about go fucking wrong.

"Isaac," Anne Marie said. "Molly. Molly...make him scream."

He turned his gaze to Anne Marie, mumbling something beneath the tape.

Anne Marie stepped back and watched as Molly, knife in hand, slide off the bed, and quiet as a mouse, slid the razor-sharp blade across each of Isaac's Achille's tendons.

Isaac thrashed upon the bed. Tears spilled from his horrified eyes.

"Molly's wanted to meet you for some time."

He tried to speak, but it was useless.

"Oh, dear Isaac, you've never had anything to say. Why bother now?"

Molly climbed from beneath the bed and stood at her side. Molly craned her head up.

Anne Marie nodded.

The doll, holding the blood-covered blade, started toward the bed.

Shaking his head back and forth, trying to buck himself free, Isaac squirmed in terror as the doll pressed the blade to his throat and drew a crimson smile across his tanned flesh.

"Molly, can I trust you to take care of the girls?"

The doll looked back and nodded.

"Good. I'm going to have a little fun of my own. Meet me back in the room in an hour."

Anne Marie left Molly to take care of Isaac. She headed toward the elevator.

***

Caleb slammed the phone down.

*Fucking, Stephen, that piece of shit.*

Thanks to that jerk off, Caleb would be pulling a double. The asshole claimed he'd severely sprained his ankle while trying to help a man being attacked in Capitol Park. That was bullshit. The guy didn't have a brave bone in his body. More likely, the fucking loser twisted his ankle trying to catch a fucking Pokémon with his phone. Caleb couldn't count the times Stephen had tried to engage him in conversations about that ridiculous waste of time app.

Caleb was about to pick up his comic when Anne Marie sauntered up to the desk.

She held her room keys at chest level, her cleavage redirecting Caleb's brain.

"Sorry, my keys aren't working. I feel like an idiot. I might have had them next to my phone." She reached into her blouse and freed the phone from her bra. Her nipple reappeared. "Oh, my god, I am so..." She fixed her bra and shirt.

"It's all... It's all right. I can make you new ones." He couldn't stop his eyes from returning to her chest if he had a .44 kissing his temple.

"Actually," she said, placing her hand on his, "I was hoping you'd bring your master key up. Just to make sure I get in. I don't want to have to come...back down again."

*Holy shit.*

He fumbled for his master key and gave it a half second's thought: escort her to her room with the intentions of promptly returning to the desk and keeping this job, or follow her into her room, see what she has to offer, and, in the worst-case scenario, get canned.

"Yeah, of course. Lead the way," he said.

As he came around the desk, she hooked his arm. "I thought you didn't like me."

"Nah, what? You're one of our best guests."

They reached the elevator. Caleb pressed the button. Her perfume was intoxicating.

"I probably wasn't so nice myself," she said.

Arm in arm, they entered the elevator. Before the doors even slid shut, she threw herself on him, slamming him against the wall. Her tongue in his mouth, her hand pressed against his dress pants. He kissed his job goodbye.

*Fuck it.*

*Thank you, Stephen.*

***

Donna whispered "Sixty-nine" into Lizzy's ear.

Lizzy didn't hesitate to crawl around the bed and offer her wet pussy to Donna's face.

Donna let her tongue go to work, somewhat shocked but equally turned on by how quick her padawan had plunged into the world of girl on girl. And goddamn was she a fast learner. Donna squeaked as the young woman pressed into her and flicked away at her clitoris like a snake in the grass. She had Lizzy's delicious juices all over her face when the door to the room opened and the lights died.

Donna eased away from Lizzy. Lizzy did the same, as both women scurried to cover themselves with the bed sheet.

The door closed and left them in complete darkness.

"Hello?" Donna said. "Anne Marie? Is that you?"

She couldn't think of anyone else it could be, but how and why she would have a key...

Lizzy yelped as she disappeared from the bed.

"Lizzy, are you all right?"

The silence of the moment was shattered by thick, gurgling sounds coming from the floor.

"Lizzy?"

Donna prided herself on having the upper hand in every situation she encountered, like with Lizzy, like with any man she chose, even with Anne Marie, letting her co-worker believe she was the Queen Bee in their hive, but Donna knew better. Now, that confidence was seeping out at warp speed.

She reached for the lamp on the nightstand and screamed as something sharp punctured her wrist. Whatever it was went in one side of her wrist, came out the other, and then was pulled back out. It happened in seconds. She pulled her arm to her chest and felt the warmth of her blood spill between her tits and down to her navel.

"Please, who's there?"

She heard someone shuffle around the bed. She didn't dare reach for the light again.

"Lizzy," she whimpered. "Help me."

She was stabbed just beneath the ribs.

She cried out and tumbled toward her assailant, falling to the floor. Her face smacked against the thin rug.

"Please," she cried quietly.

Her wails filled the room as she was punctured like a pin cushion, over and over, in the breast, the shoulder, the neck. A blinding wave of pain swallowed her whole as the blade entered her eye and shoved through to her brain.

***

Anne Marie let Caleb open the door, and then she tackled him to the bed.

Caleb's body tingled from head to toe in anticipation as she opened his pants and slipped her hand past the waistband of his underwear, wrapping her hand around his stiff cock and stroking him to the point of madness.

"Oh my God, fuck," he mumbled through his gritted teeth.

"Yeah," she said. "You like that?"

"Fuck, yes."

"I'm going to give you a night you'll never forget," she said.

He felt like he was going to explode in her hand. Caleb crawled back, trying not to cum too fast like a goddamn chump.

She freed her hand, slithered down his body, pulled his cock free, and took it in her mouth.

Caleb had never felt such intensity in any of his previous sexual experiences. His thoughts flew from corner to corner as his hands clenched the comforter beneath him. He cried out in ecstasy, delirious as he spurted again and again.

She swallowed every drop, leaving him spasming on his back, his eyes closed, a smile smeared to his face, sweating and on the verge of giggling like a schoolgirl.

Caleb put his hands over his eyes and breathed a sigh. He didn't look up until he heard the door open and close.

Sitting up, he couldn't believe his eyes. "What the...?"

The doll reached up and took Anne Marie's hand.

"Caleb, meet Molly."

She'd talked about this doll since the first week she began staying at the hotel. Molly was a bit of running joke around the back office. Even Justin and Angie had fun with it. They'd claimed to have seen Molly, but Caleb never had until now.

He stared at Molly. She was the "child" he'd seen in the window, the silhouette next to Anne Marie last night. And she was *alive*. "Jesus, what is she?"

Anne Marie, ignoring his question, bent and met the doll's dead gaze. "Molly," she said. "He's all yours. Just remember, you need to clean up your mess."

With that, Anne Marie opened the door, offered him one last sinister smile, and left them alone.

Caleb's psyche could not get around the vision standing before him. The fucking doll was alive. Then he noticed the bloody knife in Molly's hand. His gaze travelled to the crimson splotches on the doll's filthy white dress. Caleb hastily buttoned his pants and crawled across the bed to the phone on the nightstand.

Who the fuck was he going to call? *He* was supposed to be at the desk.

He heard shuffling and looked back at the entrance. Molly was gone. Holding the phone like a weapon, he scanned the room.

This was fucked.

He was fucked.

How many times do you hear *never get involved with your guests?* And he never had. The one time... He still couldn't believe it had even happened. Caleb hated Anne Marie, and yet...

"Fuck!" Caleb cried out as the knife sunk into his thigh.

The goddamn doll was going to kill him. He reached down to snatch the thing by its yarn-like yellow hair when it pulled the knife free and swiped at him. The blade ran across his wrist, splattering the wall by the phone with his blood. He drew his hand back and flung himself across the bed and to the floor.

*I'm gonna bleed out.*

Trying to get up, his legs buckled. His attempt to catch himself failed as well, thanks to his bleeding wrist. Caleb hit the floor and wanted to cry. Woozy and weak, it all happened so damned fast.

Molly appeared above him. Her button eyes had changed. The plastic pieces that had been sewn there had melted into two black pools, pulsing and swirling with death.

He had just enough time to bring his good arm up as she dropped down. The knife clutched in her hands entered one side of his forearm and came out the other, driving against his chest. Her weight was impossible. It felt like there was a boulder on top of him. He felt the tip of the weapon pierce his pectoral muscle and prayed it wouldn't hit his heart or lungs. Despite the pain, he forced himself to roll. The move knocked Molly off balance and to the floor.

Gritting his teeth, Caleb stood, the tip of the blade came free from his chest as he hobbled toward the door with the knife sticking through his arm. He glanced down at the wet stain blossoming beneath his light blue work shirt.

*I'm gonna die. I'm gonna die.*

He reached the door and tried to press the handle with his elbow. A sharp pain exploded in the back of his calf. Caleb screamed and fell backward, the door handle racing away from him.

The wind was knocked from his lungs as he hit the floor.

Molly stood. Blood, *his* blood, smeared across her face. Moaning, his head swimming in a fog of blood-loss, Caleb watched as the creature's mouth opened wide and slammed its needle-like teeth into his throat.

***

Anne Marie went behind the front desk in the lobby. She pulled up Isaac's room on the desk computer and hit the checkout button. She did the same with Lizzy and Donna. The ladies were single and wouldn't be reported missing for a few days. Isaac was a different story. His wife would be a mess, but all three would have checked out of the hotel at the same time and disappeared together. Prime suspect? The missing front desk agent that had been on duty.

Anne Marie grabbed a cup of Sleepytime tea from the coffee station and took a seat in the empty lobby. Molly needed time to finish Caleb. There would be nothing left of his body or the others. Molly never left so much as a fingernail behind. Her appetite was unrivaled.

The group's meager travel belongings would eventually be found strewn throughout the woods beyond the field out back of the hotel, but that would be another dead end. They always were.

Anne Marie and Molly had a Caribbean Cruise to catch tomorrow. A long overdue vacation, just the two of them. What kind of fun could they have out to sea?

The possibilities were endless.

# THE DEVIL'S KIN

Anna had to play this right. She needed him. The Kin needed him. When Travis heard about Arlo, he promised Anna a great reward. Recompense that would be the envy of the Kin.

The rain intensified. Her patience thinned.

"We will be safe. They even have a PlayStation 4 with every Lego game you can imagine."

"Lego Worlds?" he asked, his voice barely audible in the pounding deluge.

"Uh-huh, you bet. Now, c'mon," she said. "We can get there, get warm and dry, and get you some hot cocoa. What do you say?"

He let go and started past her in the direction they'd been heading before.

The wicked smile she hid from most crept over her face.

They were soaked to the bone as the house appeared through the trees.

Arlo stormed up the porch steps and tried to open the door.

"Hey," she shouted. "Don't be rude. We have to knock."

He grunted, his fists clenched and hanging at his sides.

She gave three firm knocks and stepped back.

Travis's smiling face welcomed them in.

She couldn't stop grinning at him. Those laser blue eyes cut through her. His long mane of deep brown hair matched his full beard and his perfect mouth. He'd kissed her last night. She tried to give herself to him, but he told her the time wasn't right. It only made her want him more.

He put something on his tongue and motioned for her to come to him. She nearly melted as he kissed her and passed the tiny pill of X to her before letting her go.

"So," he said, his voice like velvet. "This is Arlo."

Her brother stood, dripping next to her on the welcome mat.

"Hi, young man," Travis said.

"He doesn't look anybody in the eyes," Anna said. "It's a thing."

"No worries," Travis said. "Heather, Red...take our friend upstairs. Give him whatever he wants. Maybe a towel for starters."

The dark-haired twins, both petite and very pretty, joined them and offered Arlo their hands.

"He doesn't like touching people," Anna said. "But he does like video games and hot cocoa."

"Anna said you have Lego Worlds. I want to play that," Arlo said.

"Come on then," the twin on the right said. "We have it all set up and ready to go."

Arlo followed them.

Anna nearly gasped when the other twin, who had a red streak in her black hair, slyly picked up a knife from the end table next to the stairs and followed.

"Thank you for bringing him to us." Travis took her face in his hands and stared deeply into her eyes. She could feel the drug already enhancing her senses.

"Are you going to do it now?" Anna asked.

He nodded. "Do you wish to watch?"

"Yes."

Anna followed Travis up to the play room.

Still soaking wet, Arlo sat on his knees before the large television, waiting for the video game to load.

Red played with the knife between her teeth. The other twin reached behind the blue sofa lined up against the far wall. It was happening.

Travis stood behind Anna, wrapping her in his powerful arms. Every particle of her flesh felt like it was opening like a flower. She wanted him to touch all of her.

The other twin, Heather, rose up with an axe in her hands.

Anna's breath quickened. The room was electric with anticipation. Her mind swirled with it. Three other members of the Kin—Gonzo, Killian, and Tao—filed into the room and stood next to her and Travis. All were present and accounted for as Heather raised the axe.

Arlo never saw a thing. The axe swung in a perfect arc. The game controller fell to the plastic covered floor; his decapitated head thudding down next to him.

Red was on him in a heartbeat. Cutting his shirt away and plunging the blade into his small chest.

Anna was dizzy with a fever. She'd never experienced anything like it.

"Thank you," Travis whispered in her ear. His smooth voice tickled every fiber of her body.

The twins approached, holding Arlo's heart in their hands, offered it to Anna. She accepted the first bite.

"Killian!" one of the twins shouted.

"Get him, and bring him back here," Travis said.

Anna, lost in her own moment, gnawed at the warm heart like it was the greatest tasting meal she'd ever been given. The ecstasy was now in full effect. She heard the girls and now the others shouting after Killian.

Travis placed his hand on her shoulder and whispered, "Enough."

She handed the heart to him and watched him suck from the organ. His eyes rolled into the back of his head as he dropped to his knees and let the heart roll to the floor.

The others barged into the room, Tao and Gonzo dragging a kicking and screaming Killian over next to where Arlo's body lay.

Travis wiped his lips with his forearm and rose. "Hillary, hand me the axe."

Gonzo had Killian in a headlock. Killian's pale face was turning blue.

"Hold his arm," Travis ordered.

Tao stepped over Killian and pinned his wrist to the floor with his knee.

"Killian, my love... What did we talk about?" Travis said to him. "Did I not make you a promise? I knew it might come to this." He stepped to Killian's left, axe in hand, and dropped to one knee to look the skinny man in the eyes. "So, tell me, do you want to stay with us, pray with us, and proceed doing our Lords work? Hmm?"

Anna sat on her knees, rubbing her bloody hands up and down her arms, feeling as if she were enchanted.

"Let him speak," Travis ordered Gonzo. The muscle-bound, long-haired brute loosened the arm around Killian's neck. "So, Killian, my child, what's it gonna be? Will you stay or shall you go?"

"St-st-stay," he sputtered.

"Very well." Travis stood. "Hold him tight, boys."

Gonzo clenched his arm around Killian's throat. "I need to make sure you're as committed as the rest of us, Killian. So, I am going to have to exact some punishment. Are you ready?"

"Please, I won't—

"You already did," Travis shouted in Killian's face.

Killian broke into tears. "I'm suh-suh-sorry."

"You must pay a forfeit, and that forfeit must be substantial. Tao, give me his arm."

Anna looked from one face to another. Her heart raced. This was exhilarating.

"No, please," Killian pleaded.

Tao stretched Killian's arm out as Travis raised the axe over his head. There was a *woosh* as the axe swung down and severed Killian's arm just above the elbow.

Anna felt like she would drown in Killian's screams. And drowning would only let her reach her next phase—Travis's top mermaid. Life was a fucked-up dream, and the Devil's Kin were doing His work.

***

Two weeks later, Anna, Heather, and Hilary—or Red, as she preferred to be called—were in the lobby of the Department of Health and Human Services building in Augusta, hanging up flyers for their new endeavor. It had been Anna's grand idea. One that Travis applauded and the twins eagerly jumped to pursue.

*Our Children of Heaven Day Care.*

A woman in a frayed tan jacket and greasy hair stopped and stared at the poster before the girls were even out the door. "What do you think?" the woman said to the little boy at her side. She ruffled his curly blond hair and laughed. "Finally, a sitter I can afford. Looks like Mommy can get back to work." She took one of the cut strips with the house phone number and tucked it in her coat pocket.

Anna and the twins stifled their glee as they hurried outside. They had a business to run, and their first child was cute as a button. His heart would bring them one step closer to their Lord and Master.

***

Shelby tucked her son, Ben, in and kissed his forehead. "Goodnight, buddy," she whispered.

He was already fast asleep.

After a half hour phone call with her mother explaining that they had made the car payment and had enough groceries for the rest of month, thanks to their food stamp benefits, Shelby settled in with cup of tea. She'd nailed her interview at Target this afternoon and was set to start training on Monday. Thanks to the young ladies on Piggy Lane, Ben would have an affordable place to go while she made some actual money. They'd be on their feet in no time. She was looking forward to being able to pay the rent on their efficiency apartment on time for a change. It was a modest goal, but it was one that made her feel good.

She finished her tea and laid down next to her little boy.

*Our Children of Heaven.*

*A Godsend.* That was her last thought before she dozed off.

***

Monday rolled around quick. Shelby found herself struggling with Ben's bag, certain she would forget something. He was almost five and would be starting school at the end of summer, but he still held these two items near and dear to his little heart. She never wanted him to grow up.

Day care was one step closer.

She'd never been away from him outside of leaving him with Kenneth before he passed or with Grammy Marie or Mama Janice. She wasn't worried that he'd have any trouble seeing her leave. Ben was on the spectrum; he had Asperger's. He was highly functional and going new places didn't seem to bother him in the least.

It'd been almost half a year since Kenneth's sudden death. He'd had a seizure in the middle of the night and was dead before the ambulance arrived.

She had Ben buckled into his car seat and getting ready to duck into the front seat when her cellphone rang. It was Grammy Marie,

Kenneth's mother. She really didn't want to run through the day care conversation again. The woman had already given her an earful when she mentioned the place two nights ago. She knew Marie would be more than happy to watch him, but Ken Sr. was a handful. The man's diabetes had taken his sight, and last winter his condition led to the amputation of his right foot. Top it off with trips to Lewiston for dialysis treatments since his kidneys had gone to hell and Shelby didn't want to add a five-year-old to it all.

Looking at the picture of Marie, she knew she had to suck it up and answer. Marie paid for her cell service, at least until she could cover it herself, which would hopefully be soon now that she had a new job.

"Hello, Marie."

"Good morning, Shelby. Tell me I caught you before you took our boy to those strangers."

Shelby bit her tongue. She needed to stand her ground and leave no room for Marie to force the issue.

"Marie, we talked about this."

"I know, but there's no way—"

"Marie, I'm taking him to the day care and that's final."

"But you can't just leave him—"

"No. It's final. Ben will be fine. And they're even a religious group to boot."

She felt certain playing to Marie's Jesus angle would help make the woman acquiesce. *Our Children of Heaven* had to be a good ol' Christian group, right?

Marie harrumphed on the other end of the line. Shelby knew she was still irritated and probably shaking her head and knocking all her curlers out, but there was only one way to approach the woman-firm and straight.

"He'll be okay. Besides, it's only a training day for me. He'll be there just past lunch. I'll have him back in my arms by naptime."

Silence.

"Oh, all right, but please consider my offer, dear."

"Marie, please. I've got it taken care of. If things change and I need someone, you're first on the list."

Shelby got behind the steering wheel and turned the ignition.

"I expect a phone call to let me know how it went as soon as your home."

"I promise," Shelby said.

She drove out to Route 126, looking for Humphry Road. She'd never been out that way but found it easy enough. Locating Piggy Lane, on the other hand, was threatening to make her late for her first day of work. She didn't need to make a shitty impression.

Ben remained silent throughout the ride. He could speak but just chose not to most of the time. She and Kenneth had been concerned, but Dr. Hobart promised it was nothing to get too worked up about. Some kids just progressed a little slower. No two children were the same.

Shelby's mother was certain the doctors had caused Ben's condition. And when Shelby's sister, Kelly, heard this, she started regurgitating the anti-vaxxer nonsense, saying how the almighty Jenny fucking McCarthy had warned everyone not to give into to all these unnecessary vaccines. Shelby did not subscribe to such complete and utter bullshit.

Ben was a normal learner; he was just quieter than most. Her family's affinity for drama and through the roof paranoia was tiring. Which is why when she did let someone watch Ben it was usually Marie. The woman was pushy, but at least she wasn't prone to bouts of insanity. Marie was a former judge. She had her shit together. She could sense BS half the world away.

*So why didn't you listen to her today?*

True, Marie telling her she couldn't trust complete strangers with Ben had caused tendrils of unease to explore Shelby's stomach, but the need to prove she could handle her family on her own meant something to her. She needed to do this.

Lost in thought, Shelby slammed the brakes. She'd nearly missed the tiny dirt road. The Piggy Lane sign was handmade. She backed up and turned onto the skinny road that was barley big enough for her Escort. As she pulled up to the house, she was both relieved and nervous about being the only one there.

Looking in the rearview, Ben was gazing out the window. "You ready, buddy?"

He met her gaze in the mirror and shook his head from side to side. It hit her heart like a bullet.

"Aw, it's only for a few hours, baby boy. Mommy has to work. Come on," she said. "Let's go meet the other kiddos."

He gave a slight smile at that. He didn't say much to adults, but she had heard him chat with kids his own age whenever they went to the McDonald's with the playhouse.

He held her hand as they made their way to the front door. They didn't even make it when the door opened, and the twins welcomed them with smiles.

"Hi. Oh my God, who is this handsome little devil?" the one with a red streak in her hair said, bending down and holding her hand out to Ben.

"Ben, go on and say hello," Shelby said.

"Hello," he said.

Shelby thought she even saw a grin crack his face. *Hmm.*

"I'm Heather, and we are going to have so much fun while your mommy is at work. I promise. Are you ready?"

Ben looked up at Shelby. She nodded. He smiled wider than she could remember him doing in some time.

He met Heather's gaze and nodded. Heather took his hand and led him inside.

"Hillary, but everyone calls me, Red," the young woman said. "And please don't worry about a thing. He's in great hands, Ms. Hines. Go on now; we wouldn't want you to be late for your first day."

Shelby had meant to get here early enough to check the inside of the place out and make sure everything was up to her standards, but knowing she was up against the clock, and seeing the way Ben lit up in Heather's presence made her feel much better.

"Okay. Thank you guys so much. If you need me, you have my number, right?"

"We won't need a thing," Red said. "And yes, I have it right here." She held up the online form Shelby had filled out last week.

It seemed almost like she was blocking the doorway now, but Shelby told herself she was letting her family's paranoia infect her. "Okay. Can I just say bye to him?"

Red looked back and shook her head. "We have a video game station upstairs that the kids go crazy for. Looks like he's already followed my sister up."

"Oh...I guess just tell him for me?"

"I will. Bye, Ms. Hines."

And just like that, her boy was in the hands of people she didn't really know. She looked at her cell. 7:46.

*Shit.* She had fourteen minutes to get to Augusta.

She rushed to the car and turned around in the empty driveway and headed to work.

***

"Um, my mom told me..."

"Yes, go ahead, Ben," Heather said, holding his hand.

"She told me there would be other kids here."

"Oh, we did have one other boy, but he's not coming today," Anna said as she brought a tray of Goldfish and apple juice to the coffee table.

"Oh." His chin dropped to his skinny chest.

"He's not coming any day," Red said, chuckling on her way by them.

Anna struck her in the thigh.

"Ow," Red said.

Anna glared at her, and said, "Be good."

"Do you like to play video games," Heather asked.

He shook his head.

"No?" Heather said. "Well, we have some of the coolest ones. Do you ever play with Legos?"

He nodded.

Red hopped over to the shelf with the games on it. "No way, we should let him play Doom!"

"Red, sit down," Anna said.

"Why should I? Because the princess said so?"

Anna knew Red's resentment for her was boiling up. It had gotten worse this weekend when Travis had kicked the twins out of his bedroom and only let Anna sleep with him now.

"Maybe you should go downstairs for a bit," Anna said.

"Yeah, Red, stop being such a fucking bitch," Heather said.

Ben dropped his gaze to the floor.

"Especially in front of sweet Ben here." Heather patted his knee.

"Well, Ben," Red said, putting the game with the monster on the cover down in front of the Goldfish. "You get to murder the fuck out of monsters in this one. It's fucking awesome."

Anna stood and pointed at the stairs. "Get out, right now."

"You think this great idea of yours is going to keep you in his bed? You aren't the first, honey."

Anna wanted to smash the bitch in the mouth but kept herself in check as Red finally strolled out of the room.

"I am so sorry about her, Ben," Anna said. "Red is having a really bad day. We'll keep her out of here, okay?"

"He's trembling," Heather said.

Anna picked Doom up from the table and tossed it out of sight. "We don't have to play video games. Do you want to watch *Finding Nemo*?"

He peeked up at her and then nodded. He was tense now, his hands folded on his knees. His little lip was trembling.

Anna didn't really give a fuck that he was suddenly nervous. He wasn't going home after lunch, or ever again, but damn it if Red didn't fucking like to make things so much more complicated. Things went much easier when they all worked together and kept the kids happy or at least somewhat comfortable until Travis and the boys got up.

Heather stayed with Ben as Anna got the movie started. After the first fifteen minutes or so, Ben began to snack on the Goldfish.

*Good.*

Unlike Red the Cunt, Heather was terrific with the children. She was born for this.

"I'm going to go fix up some brunch," Anna said. "Ben, would you like some cereal or toast?"

"No thank you," he said.

"Heather? Anything for you?"

"No thank you," she said, smiling and squeezing the boy's hand. Ben smiled too. She was so fucking good with them.

"Okay. Be good, you two," Anna said. She stepped from the game room and walked down the dim hallway toward Travis's room.

He lay naked and uncovered. She stared at his beautiful form and thought of the way he'd fucked her last night. He truly was a beast in human form. And she was the luckiest girl in the world.

He should come to within the hour, and then they could bring him to meet the next sacrifice. He would devour the third heart in as many weeks. Her plan was working brilliantly, and she had finally been rewarded. Thinking of the look in his eyes when he took the boy's heart thrilled her to the core of her damned soul.

***

An hour and a half into her training and Shelby hadn't retained a thing. She could not concentrate. She'd made it to work with one minute to spare. However, since punching in her team member number, she hadn't been able to stop kicking herself for not saying bye to Ben. She couldn't stop imagining him sitting in a corner by himself, scared, and the girl's not letting him go to the bathroom.

Her trainer, a tall skinny girl named Jenny, was rambling on about one policy or another when Shelby pulled the piece of paper with the day care's phone number on it from her pocket.

"Excuse me," Shelby said. "Can I go to the bathroom?"

"Oh, yeah, sure. It's out the door and the first door on the right."

"Thanks," she said.

Shelby hurried out and into the bathroom. She pulled out her cell and punched the number in. The phone rang five times before someone finally picked up.

"Hello?" Shelby said.

The line clicked, and she was met with a dial tone. They'd answered and hung up on her. What the hell?

She tried the number again. This time she was hung up on after only two rings. Something was wrong.

Bursting from the restroom, she didn't even bother heading back to let Jenny know she was leaving. She tried the number again. This time it rang endlessly.

In her car and speeding toward Route 126, she prayed Ben was all right.

***

Killian had done his best to stay away when the girls had their kids. He didn't want to leave Travis, but that didn't mean he had to watch their horror show. He just prayed the Devil would accept him for his endurance, his perseverance, his dedication. Looking down at the stump where his elbow should be, he thought of another word. His sacrifice.

The air was refreshing out here. He'd moved from Portland up to the tiny Litchfield community and had truly felt blessed finding Travis and Gonzo. They'd taken him in, showed him the Devil's love, and finally made him feel like he belonged somewhere. There was no judgement. And when they'd killed the first two men, the homosexual couple from the diner, a sense of electricity crackled through his whole body. The woman from the Walmart parking lot was next. And that's where things began to really get good. They brought the twins in and then they were able to lure even more sacrifices in from the college. It was when they introduced the first child to the house that Killian faltered.

Travis had said that Satan told him sacrificing the young and innocent would help them achieve the ultimate closeness to Him, but Killian knew it had been the twins' idea. He'd heard them whisper it to Travis after a drug-induced orgy. The next day the girls brought home the child, stolen right from his front yard. They were high when they slaughtered him and carved out his heart.

Killian threw up.

Travis had taken him in his arms that night and then into his bed. Just him. Killian explained how the child sacrifice had made him uncomfortable. Travis told him he understood, but that the Devil demanded it, and that they were to do what needed to be done. He promised it would get easier, and Killian desperately wanted to believe him.

When Anna came in with her brother, it was not easier. It was far worse. So he'd run. He didn't plan on leaving for good. He just needed space to think. When they dragged him back inside, Travis didn't allow him the chance to explain. Looking at his arm again, he knew Travis had to do it. And while Killian cried and still didn't agree with the new path the girls had led them down, his love for Travis had only grown, and thus his commitment to the Kin, his only family.

He was about to make his way inside the house when he saw the car blazing up the driveway. It was the mother from this morning. She knew. Somehow she knew her son was not safe here. He hurried back to the house.

Killian felt himself faltering again.

***

Anna was sitting next to Ben on the sofa eating her Cocoa Pebbles when Red barged into the room. Something was wrong. "Sit tight, Ben. Heather?"

Heather looked nervous, but she nodded and took Anna's spot next to the boy. If he noticed the sudden tension in the air, it didn't show. His eyes were locked on the animated movie on the screen. She followed Red out the door, closing it behind her.

"Killian says the mother is here." Red was holding the large kitchen knife.

The sound of tires crunching up the gravel driveway was unmistakable.

Anna opened the door and motioned for Heather to join her. Once she did, she closed the door again. "The mother is back. We'll try to convince her everything is fine, but it might not go so well. Be ready."

"We should wake the men," Red said.

"No," Anna said, placing a hand on her shoulder. "We need to prove to Travis that we can take care of things. We'll try to talk her down. If we have to kill her, then we do it."

Together, they met the distraught mother at the door.

"I want to see Ben," Shelby said.

"Is everything okay?" Anna asked.

"My training was just shorter than I thought it would be. Will you go get Ben please."

"He's actually napping at the moment," Red said. "Why don't you come in and have a coffee or tea. I'm sure he'll be up soon enough."

Shelby tried to push past the girls.

"Hey," Red said. "You can't just barge in here."

Shelby was in a panic. If they didn't get this shit shut down quick the men would be up.

"Shelby," Anna said, as calmly as she could. "Look, I get it, you're nervous about leaving Ben alone for the first time. We see it every week. But he's fine. Heather is sitting with him. He fell asleep watching *Finding Nemo* in the game room." She looked at her watch. "He's been out maybe thirty minutes now. Have a seat and I'll grab us some coffee. If you still want to check in on him, I'll be glad to take you upstairs."

***

*Oh my God. I must seem like a complete spaz.* Shelby relaxed, slightly. Glancing around the room, nothing appeared out of the ordinary. There was a box of Frosted Flakes and Cocoa Pebbles on the counter, clean dishes drying on a rack, and the Beatles playing from an old, giant piece of furniture in the living room that looked more like a bureau than a record player. She turned her attention to the stairs leading to the second floor, the game room, Ben.

"Is it okay if I start the kettle for some tea?" Anna asked.

"I'm so sorry," Shelby said. "That'd be nice."

Red led her to the brown sofa. Shelby still didn't quite like this girl. Out of the three, there was something in this one's eyes that she didn't trust. Something feral. Shelby took a seat as Anna joined them.

"He's really been great," Anna said, smiling. "A lot of the kids like video games, but Ben just wanted to chill with a movie. Before any of us knew it, he'd fallen asleep."

"How are the others?" Shelby said.

"The others?" Red asked.

"The other kids? You guys do have more than Ben, don't you?"

"The other little boy, Allan," Anna said, "he wasn't feeling good this morning, so his mother kept him home. And Sally is away this week at a summer camp. I think it was a Bible school thing, right, Red?"

"So it's just Ben and your sister up there?"

"Uh-huh," Red replied

"I'm sure he's fine, but maybe I should just let him know I'm here."

Shelby started to get up as the kettle began to whistle. As Shelby turned toward the stairs, a man with a stump at his elbow appeared from the second floor and started down. His face twisted in a grimace. He was sweaty and uncomfortable. That bad feeling came thundering back like a dam of stupidity had just given way.

The man gave Shelby a pitiful glance as he hurried past them and out the front door.

"That was—" Red started

"Our brother, Killian," Anna interrupted. "He's been staying with us since coming home from Afghanistan. It's been hard for him, the transition back to normalcy and with his injury and all."

"Oh," Shelby said. She felt like she was on an emotional roller coaster. "I'm sorry to hear that, but I think I should still get Ben. This morning's been a real doozy for me, and I think I'd just feel better if we went home."

"Of course," Anna said, turning to her sister. "Red, will you bring Shelby up to the game room?"

"Follow me," Red said, tiptoeing barefoot up the stairs.

The kettle's shrill whistle, the barefoot girl with the feral eyes, the worried man with half an arm, her anxiety about still not seeing Ben, it all suddenly overwhelmed her. She felt lightheaded as she grasped the banister.

"Are you okay?" Anna asked, placing a hand on her back.

"I just want my boy," Shelby whispered.

"I'm sorry," Anna said into her ear, "but you should have just come back when you were supposed to."

"What?"

Shelby didn't see the punch coming. Anna's fist connected with her temple, and the girl suddenly gripped her hair and began slamming Shelby's head against the wall. Everything happened too fast, but Shelby tried to get her arms up for protection. Anna was laughing now as she continued her assault. Shelby heard the damn whistle from the kettle more like siren, or a warning now. She'd been right to come back, but was she already too late?

She threw a blind elbow at Anna and caught her in the nose. Blood exploded down the insane woman's face, but she only grinned behind a crimson smear.

Shelby forced herself forward, going in for a second strike as Red came storming past Anna and closelined Shelby, taking her right off her feet. She landed flat on her back at the bottom of the stairs, the air knocked from her lungs.

*Ben, I have to get to Ben.*

Red sat upon her chest holding a giant kitchen knife.

The man, the brother, came back inside. "What are you doing?" he asked.

"Go get Travis and the boys," Red ordered.

"No," Anna said. "We've got this under control."

"Bitch, you are not the goddamn leader around here. Killian, go get Travis."

Killian dropped his chin and started upstairs.

"Please," Shelby cried, grazing his leg with her hand as he hurried by her.

He glanced down, meeting her gaze. There was something in his eyes, just a glimmer. He gave the slightest of nods and carried on. She saw him reaching for the blade sheathed on his belt.

"Now, it's time to deal with you," Red said, that full-bestial gaze turned up to ten and bearing down on Shelby.

A loud crack knocked the look right out of the woman's eyes as she fell forward. The knife dropped to the floor next to Shelby's head as Red slumped like a rag doll over her. Anna stood behind her holding a baseball bat. The damned whistle still screamed in the background.

"What have you done," another voice from upstairs called down.

Anna turned around. As soon as she did, Shelby shoved Red's motionless body to the floor and grabbed the knife. She didn't hesitate as she plunged the blade into Anna's calf muscle. Anna cried out and fell. Shelby grabbed the bat, holding it like a samurai sword.

She charged the other twin at the top of the stairs, chasing Heather into the game room, where the twin stopped dead in her tracks. Heather stepped over to Ben standing in front of a large television.

"Mama," he said.

Heather had an axe in her hand.

"I wanna go home," he said.

"Don't touch him," Shelby said, entering the room, ready to throw the bat at this bitch's head if she had to.

"He's been chosen, and you fucking delivered him to us."

"Ben, everything's going to be okay," Shelby said, fighting back the tears.

"Travis!" Heather shouted. "Tao! Gonzo! Get your asses in here right fucking now!"

Ben lurched forward, but Heather grabbed him by the wrist and jerked him back to her, clutching him by the back of the neck. Ben's tears broke Shelby's heart.

Killian stood in the doorway. The knife in his hand dripped fresh blood to the floor. He had it all over him.

"What the hell did you do?" Heather said. "Travis!"

"Give her the boy, Heather," Killian said.

Shelby saw the shock in the crazy bitch's face. She charged the woman and swung the baseball bat before Heather could get the axe up. The bat caught the girl flush in the cheek with an audible crack. Ben had ducked away, but now wrapped himself against Shelby's hips. Heather collapsed to the floor, her arms waving out at them.

"Take your son and get out of here. Go now," Killian said.

"Thank you," Shelby said.

He stepped aside and allowed them to pass.

Bloody faced and limping, knife in hand, Anna made her way to the middle of the stairs, blocking their way out. "You shouldn't have done that, Shelby. Now you're going to fucking pay."

"Get behind Mama, Ben," Shelby said.

"No, I wanna go home. Please, mama," he cried.

"Get out of their way, Anna," Killian said.

"Fuck you, Killian, you traitor. Travis showed you mercy, and this is how you repay him? Well, it's not going to work. They're already dead, and you're next when the boys... Wait, what did you do to Heather?" Anna's eyes took in his blood-soaked shirt.

"They're dead, Anna," he said. "All of them."

"No, you lie. You're a fucking liar. Travis! Travis!"

Shelby and Ben backed away.

Anna growled as limp and all, she charged up the stairs. Killian met her at the top step with a boot to her face sending her flying backwards.

Shelby clutched Ben and picked him up, holding him on her hip.

"Please, go," Killian said. "I'm so sorry, but you have to get away from here."

"Thank you," she said. And with that she hurried down the stairs past the two crumpled bodies of Red and Anna. Anna's hand twitched as they passed her, but she otherwise did not move.

Bursting out into the high noon sun, Shelby got Ben into the car and buckled him next to her in the front seat. "We'll get you in your seat once we get down the road. Okay, baby?" she said to him.

He nodded.

She started the car and swung the vehicle around, taking one final glance at the house of horrors before leaving the bloody hell on Piggy Lane in her rearview mirror.

***

Killian kneeled next to Anna and placed the knife on the floor. She was still breathing, but her neck was at a horrible angle. Petting her hair, he leaned down to her ear. "I only wanted to be loved. Everything was fine until you came along." Her gaze found his. "I loved him, too. And you made me kill him."

Whatever rage Anna held had been knocked out of her.

Killian sat up straight and picked up the knife. He tucked the point under his chin, tears leaking down his face. "For you Lord," he said before falling forward on the blade.

## STORY NOTES

## In the Basement of the Amazing Alex Cucumber

This is an oldie. First off, that title came about because my girls when they were younger referred to Alice Cooper as Alex Cucumber. I just had to write a story about this "Alex Cucumber" I thought it sounded like a character. In this story, he's more of a Jim Morrison meets David Koresh type of guy. Two local boys get invited to one of his affairs and the story takes over from there.

## The Dead Brother Situation

This is one of those stories that I had so much fun writing. Graeme Reynolds invited me to write a werewolf story for his anthology (*Leaders of the Pack*). The caveat was that it had to be in our already established werewolf world. I was honored to be included alongside Ray Garton, Jeff Strand, Jonathan Janz, and more. The title is a play on The Bonnie Situation (from *Pulp Fiction*). It features Nick Bruce, a werewolf from my novel *Blood and Rain*. We get a glimpse into the world Nick lives in now, and I definitely let my love for Tarantino shine through in this story. Like I said, it was a blast to write.

## Gone Away

This is a flash piece I wrote about an online friend that suffered the worst type of tragedy a parent can endure. I cried like a baby for his loss. I was moved to craft this piece. I didn't know what else I could do.

## Orson's Gas N' Go

I was invited to write a story for the Sinister Horror Group's *Black Room Manuscripts (vol. 3)*. I'm a HUGE fan of Tobe Hooper's movies *Texas Chainsaw Massacre* and *Eaten Alive*. I wanted to write a story that had that hectic, frazzled, nerve-wracking feeling like you couldn't relax because something crazy could happen any second.

## Molly

This one was for Jack Bantry's *Splatterpunk Fighting Back* charity anthology. Both the story and the anthology wound up as nominees for the Splatterpunk Awards (my story lost, but the antho won). A co-worker wanted me to write a story with him in it. I just had a fight of sorts with a group of business workers that were staying at the hotel every week and one of them had a doll named Molly that she wanted to freak out our GM with. I got over my issues with them and decided to add them all into this story (along with Molly). It's got blood and sex and all that a good Splatterpunk joint should.

## The Guide

Another short piece, I cried at the end of this one. It was originally titled "Stolen Car" after a Bruce Springsteen song, but I could never make that story work. I took the basic idea—a guy dies but doesn't realize he's dead, bumps into a guide of sorts, and figures it out. The end was just really sad for me to write. I have three children and imagined this being me.

## The Devil's Kin

I wrote this one for Silver Shamrock's *Midnight in the Pentagram* anthology, but I pulled the story back before Ken McKinley could read it. I freaked out at the start of the pandemic and didn't want anyone having to pay me for any stories. In a strange twist of events, the story found its way onto Silver Shamrock here in this collection. I wrote this story after hearing about a Canadian cult leader named Roch Theriault. I heard the story on (the podcast) *My Favorite Murder* and it was so wild I just needed to write something around it. It's pretty rough and evil.

## Mourning Pictures

A friend of mine spent a year posting these ridiculously funny photos on a Facebook page he made just for doing so. They always made me laugh. He even puts his name down in the corner in a nice professional font which made it all the more hilarious. I intended to write a real spooky ghost story, but it turned out kind of precious instead.

## Everett

Okay, my mom has a very creepy collection of dolls, so dolls are a thing with me. I don't know where the idea for this one came from, but it turned freaky and twisted, and sometimes, that's my jam.

## You Can Have It All Back

What would you do if you were sick and you had the power to rid yourself of the sickness? Would you do it if it meant hurting someone else?

## Comfortably Numb

Took the title from my favorite Pink Floyd song, but this story was inspired by something I read about Japan's "Suicide Forest." The idea of such a place is unnerving and sad in so many ways.

## Kelvin's World

This story surprised me. It started off as a straightforward come-uppance type tale. An internet troll taking his self-loathing out on others runs into more trouble than he bargained for. Once I started thinking about the "victim" of this troll, it turned into a darker story.

## Out of Range

This is probably the second oldest piece in this collection. I have always loved writing about aliens, and this is probably my favorite of the batch. The title is from an Ani DiFranco song that I love, and it just set the mood for the tale I wanted to create. "They" send a message that they are coming. The next thing they do is kill the internet. I think that's just a frightening one-two punch.

## Master of Beyond

Never play with a Ouija board! This story appears in *Welcome to the Show*, a shared universe anthology from Crystal Lake Publishing. All the stories take place in a haunted venue in San Francisco. My story takes place in the 80s hair metal days. An evil demon is summoned and intends to bring forth an even more powerful and wicked force. Writing anything set in the 80s with heavy metal or hair bands is my happy place.

# ALSO BY GLENN ROLFE

**Novels:**
Blood and Rain
Becoming
The Window
Until Summer Comes Around
August's Eyes

**Novellas:**
Abram's Bridge
Things We Fear
Something in the Groove

**Collections:**
Slush
Land of Bones
Nocturnal Pursuits

# About the Author

**Glenn Rolfe** is an author from the haunted woods of New England. He has studied Creative Writing at Southern New Hampshire University and continues his education in the world of horror by devouring the novels of Stephen King, Richard Laymon, Brian Keene, Jack Ketchum, and many others. He has three children, Ruby, Ramona, and Axl. He is grateful to be loved despite his weirdness.

He is a Splatterpunk Award nominee and the author of Until Summer Comes Around, Ascension Agenda, Blood and Rain, The Window, Becoming, The Haunted Halls, Chasing Ghosts, Abram's Bridge, Things We Fear, Boom Town, and the collections, Slush and Land of Bones.

www.ingramcontent.com/pod-product-compliance
Lightning Source LLC
Chambersburg PA
CBHW051225210726
48290CB00003B/803